MIKE LUPICA

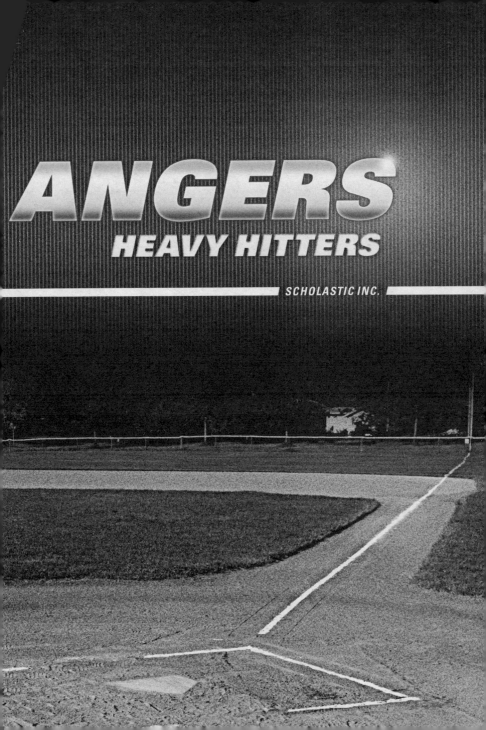

No part of this publication may be reproduced, stored in a retrieval system, or transmitted in any form or by any means, electronic, mechanical, photocopying, recording, or otherwise, without written permission of the publisher. For information regarding permission, write to Scholastic Inc., Attention: Permissions Department, 557 Broadway, New York, NY 10012.

This book was originally published in hardcover by Scholastic Press in 2014.

ISBN 978-0-545-38181-9

12 11 10 9 8 7 6 5 4 3 2 1   15 16 17 18 19 20/0

Printed in the U.S.A.   40
This edition first printing, May 2015

Book design by Phil Falco

This book is for my parents, Bene and Lee Lupica.

BOOKS BY
MIKE LUPICA

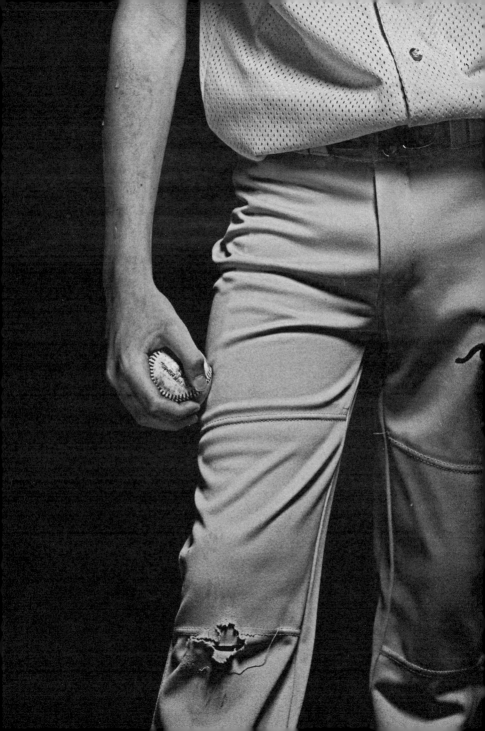

"I've made a decision," <u>Cooper Manley</u>, known as <u>Coop</u>, was saying. "I don't want to grow up."

It made <u>Ben McBain</u> smile. But then that happened a lot when Coop was around. He was funny even when he wasn't trying to be.

"I don't think it's going to be a problem for you," Ben said. "Not growing up, I mean."

<u>Sam Brown</u> said, "Not gonna lie, the rest of us just figured that you're as mature as you're ever going to get."

"But he can get more *im*mature, right?" <u>Shawn O'Brien</u> said.

"Absolutely!" Ben said. "I've got Coop's back on that one. I think he can get a *lot* more immature than he already is."

"Go ahead, make fun of me all you want," Coop said.

"Okay," Sam said.

"But you know I'm right," Coop said. "Which one of you wouldn't want to stay eleven forever?"

"I'm down with it as long as I get to grow," Ben said. The smallest of them, by a lot. "Because I'd sure like to start doing some growing one of these days."

Now Sam was the one smiling, saying, "Coop feels the exact same way about his brain."

They all laughed: Coop, Sam, Shawn. Ben McBain's three best guy friends in the world. Friends, buds, teammates. "A band of bros" is the way Coop liked to put it. When Lily Wyatt was around, they called themselves the Core Four Plus One. Shawn joined the group when he moved to town, started sixth grade with them at Rockwell Middle School, and ended up playing football and basketball with them.

It hadn't been easy with Shawn at first, especially in football, with Ben and Shawn both competing for the quarterback spot last fall. And Shawn had been handed the job first, by his dad, a former NFL quarterback coaching the team, once the greatest player to ever come out of Rockwell. But Ben had finally beaten him out. Shawn became a solid tight end for them and the Rockwell Rams ended up winning the Butler County League when Ben threw a Hail Mary pass to Sam at the end of the championship game.

As soon as football season ended, it was time for basketball to start. The Rams didn't win the championship in basketball, mostly because Sam suffered a bad ankle sprain practicing with Ben one day, and missed almost the whole regular season. But Sam had come back for the last game and they had beaten Darby — their biggest rival in just about everything except texting — to spoil Darby's undefeated season. All of them walking away from that game feeling like champs, having shown Darby and its star player Chase Braggs how things laid out when the sides were even.

Now school was out, summer was officially starting for them. The Little League season was over in Rockwell and the All-Star team had been selected for the Butler County League. Ben and Sam and Coop and Shawn had all made it. They were about to have their first practice, Sam's dad coaching them, Ben's dad assisting him, the Core Four guys sitting high up in the bleachers at Highland Park, waiting for the rest of the team to arrive. Coop was doing most of the talking, because no one could talk like Coop.

Talking about wanting to keep things the way they were right now forever. Coop so ready for another baseball season to begin that he was already wearing his shin guards, having been a catcher from the first time he and Ben and Sam had played together, when it was still their dads pitching to them.

"Just look at how good we've got it in terms of baseball," Coop said. "We already had one season, even if we were all on different teams. Now we not only get a do-over on the season, we're all together the way we were in football and basketball. And it's *summer*. And you know what summer means."

"No more Cs for you in math?" Sam said, trying to sound helpful.

Coop just gave him a disgusted look. Ben knew the deal with Coop, it was like football announcers said sometimes on television: You couldn't stop him, you only hoped to contain him.

Coop said, "Summer means we don't have to worry about

anything having to do with school — other than maybe summer reading, which I don't think about until, like, August — for almost three whole months. All we have to do is play baseball and hang out. And you know what's better than that? Nothing is better than that. Which is what I've been trying to explain to you boneheads."

"Wait, I figured it out," Shawn said. "Coop doesn't want to be Buster Posey." He was the Giants' catcher and had been the MVP and was Coop's current favorite player. "He wants to be Peter Pan."

"Actually," Sam said, "the way his mind jumps around, he does remind me a little bit of Tinker Bell."

Coop turned to Ben now and said, "Help a brother out. They'll listen to you, they always do, and I know that you know that what I'm saying makes sense."

"Some of it," Ben said.

"*Thank* you!" Coop said.

"I said some of it," Ben said. "Eleven has been a cool age, no doubt. But the way I look at it, why shouldn't we think things aren't going to get better as we get older, in sports and everything else?"

"Wait," Sam said, "does that mean Lily can get cooler than she already thinks she is?"

"Hard to believe," Ben said, "but certainly doable."

And just like that, almost on cue, they could hear Lily Wyatt's voice from behind the bleachers, Lily saying, "I'm here."

They had been swimming in Shawn's pool earlier in the afternoon and Lily had told them she might bike over and watch some of their first practice, Lily loving baseball more than any girl they knew, maybe because she was such a total star as a pitcher and hitter on her softball team. But Ben knew it wasn't just a love of baseball bringing her to Highland Park, it was the fact that the rest of the Core Four was here, and Lily was afraid she might miss something.

Fun, mostly.

The pure fun of all of them being together on a summer night like this.

She made her way up the bleachers on long legs, taking three rows at a time, waving a hand when she got to them, her way of telling Coop to slide over. Lily sat down next to Ben, and said, "What's good, Big Ben?"

It was what she called him, not as a joke, not to be sarcastic or make fun of his size, but because she was the one always telling him that the only size that mattered in sports was the size of your talent and the size of your heart. She called him Big Ben because of that, because of the kind of teammate he was.

And the kind of friend she was.

"Getting ready to play my favorite sport, Lils."

"Which means," Coop said, "whatever sport that's in season."

Lily gave Ben a long look. "What *is* your favorite, really?" she said.

"Haven't decided yet," Ben said.

"Where do you think they'll put you this season," she said, "second or short?"

"Mr. Brown says he's thinking short, my arm is wasted at second," he said. "But you want to know the truth? I don't care where I play."

Ben had played both second and short in Little League this season. And pitched in relief. Even played the outfield occasionally. To Ben, it was the beauty of baseball, at least at their age: You didn't have to be just one thing. It was different in football, Ben had always seen himself as a quarterback even when his coaches couldn't see past his lack of size and kept playing him somewhere else, before he got his chance to show everybody this past season that he had the arm and the game and the judgment to be the one thing you always wanted to be in sports:

A game changer.

In basketball he was a point guard, a better passer than he was a shooter — even though he'd beaten Darby with a last-second fallaway over Chase Braggs — and always believing that all good ball started with a good pass.

Baseball was different. You really did have to be a lot of things in baseball: Hitter, fielder, thrower, runner. All that. Ben was a born leadoff man, not because his size made him tough to pitch to, but because he could hit, had the bat speed for it, because he had the eyes to spot a pitch he could hit hard somewhere. Every year he'd surprise more people with how hard he could hit a baseball, the way he kept surprising people with how far he could throw a football.

He loved to hit, loved to pitch, loved to make a good stop and throw a guy out at first by a step. Mostly, he just loved to *play.* Loved the downtime you got in baseball between pitches when you were in the field, waiting for the moment when the ball would be in play and it seemed as if everything was happening at once, guys on the bases, decisions to be made about what to do with the ball if it was hit to you, or where you needed to be if it was hit to somebody else.

Greg Brown, Sam's dad, who'd been a star pitcher at Rockwell High and a decent player at Richmond after that, liked to say that baseball was "the greatest game ever invented by mortal minds." And sometimes on a night like this, with the grass freshly cut and the lines looking as white as they could be and the infield dirt looking as if nobody had played on this field all spring — everything looking clean and new — Ben thought that Mr. Brown might just be right.

"Basically," Ben said to Lily, "I don't care where I play as long as we win."

"Shocker," Coop said. "Totally."

Ben could see other players starting to show up now, even though practice wasn't scheduled to start for another half hour at least. Justin Bard, the middle linebacker on their football team, was walking slowly across the outfield grass with Darrelle Clayton, a fullback from football and a shooting guard from basketball, who was probably going to play left field. Darrelle was fast and good. But Justin was *great*, maybe even a better all-around baseball player than Sam was, which was saying a lot, because Sam could crush it as a center fielder and was a lock to hit third in front of Justin.

Justin Bard was a left-handed hitter with more power than

anybody in the Butler County League that Ben had ever seen, was a lock-down fielder at first base, and had a good enough arm, and enough confidence in it, to throw across the diamond and nail guys at third when the other team would try to put a bunt down on him.

As good a linebacker as Justin was, as much ground as he could cover, he was better in baseball. By a lot. Absolutely no doubt with him what *his* favorite sport was, he already talked about making it to the big leagues someday.

"You guys ready?" Ben said. "We won the league in football. Didn't win in basketball. We've gone *way* too long without a title." Smiling as he said it.

"Wow," Lily said. "What's it been, like, four whole months?"

"Hey," Sam Brown said, "you're telling me you didn't feel like we won something by beating Darby the way we did in our last game?"

"Wait," Ben said, "what did I do with the trophy they gave us for that?"

Sam said, "Aren't you the guy always telling me there's more than one way to be a winner in sports?"

Lily giggled. "I love it when one of you quotes Big Ben *to* Big Ben."

"Whatever," he said. "Here's all I'm going to say, and all I want out of this season: For nobody to get hurt the way Sam did in basketball. For nothing to happen that will keep us from being the best team we can be. If it doesn't, we'll be the best team in the league."

"I'm down with that," Coop said.

"Me, too," Sam said.

"Same," Shawn said.

Ben said, "As long as nothing bad happens, we'll be fine."

They weren't.

First league game, bottom of the last for the Rams at Highland Park, under the lights, bleachers nearly filled, Rams down a run to Parkerville, Robbie Burnett — the quarterback of the Parkerville football team and the star of their basketball team — on the mound trying to get the last three outs for his team.

Against the top of the Rams order.

Ben first, then Darrelle, then Sam, then Justin Bard.

Ben's dad coaching at first, Mr. Brown coaching at third. Ben already had two hits on this night, had just made a diving stop behind second to save a run and maybe two, keeping the Parkerville lead at just 6–5.

But they were still down a run. And nobody wanted to lose the opener. So Ben planned to get on base any way he could, set things up for the guys coming up behind him, figuring it wouldn't take much to get the inning — and the game — to Justin, the big stick in their lineup. It had been a terrible night for Justin so far, he'd struck out twice, once looking, and had made a bad error with the bases loaded, a ball behind the first-base bag going through his legs and allowing two runs to score. But nobody — maybe nobody except Justin — would remember any of that if he knocked in the winning run.

Unless Sam Brown beat him to it, of course.

As Ben put on his batting helmet, Sam said to him, "Anything better than a walk-off win in the first game?"

"Doubtful," Ben said. "And not only a walk-off, a come-from-behind walk-off."

Sam said, "He's going to want to get ahead of you."

"Coach already told me to go after the first good pitch I see."

"They haven't gotten you out all night and they're not going to do it now," Sam said. "You'll score the tying run and then either Darrelle or me scores the winner."

"Well," Ben said, "when you make it sound so simple."

"Just trying not to confuse you."

"Basically what I'm hearing is that you'd like me to get on base," Ben said.

"You really are practically a genius," Sam said as Ben walked toward the plate, no batting gloves, he was old-school about almost everything in sports.

Robbie Burnett looked to be about twice Ben's size standing on the mound. He not only looked like he was a high school kid, he threw as hard as one, a big right-handed beast whose only pitch was a fastball because he didn't need anything else.

Ben wasn't afraid of Robbie or his fastball, or a moment like this, this is why you played, for moments like this. What was there to be afraid of? If you didn't want to be up with the game on the line, when did you?

Ben wasn't afraid, period.

He tapped their catcher's shin guards with his bat. Took his stance. Dug in with his back shoe, putting most of his weight back there. Set his bat high the way his dad had always taught him. There was chatter from behind him, from the Rams' bench, but Ben could barely hear it, things always got quiet for Ben in moments like this, he was just locked in on Robbie, waiting for the first-pitch fastball he knew was coming.

Robbie's best against his best, straight up, Robbie rocking into his motion, not much of a leg kick, just his right arm coming forward, Ben keeping his eyes on the ball as it came out of his hand, knowing the ball was going to get on him in a blink, but somehow feeling as if the game was slowing down for him at the same time.

Maybe Robbie just flat overthrew the ball. Or maybe he was fixed on throwing one right past Ben, getting ahead on the count.

But the pitch got away from him, the ball tailing in on Ben before he could do much to react, before he could do much more than spin to his left, his spikes catching in the dirt, Ben stumbling and falling backward, out of the batter's box as he did, trying to get away from the ball.

Just not soon enough.

The ball caught him flush on the inside of his left arm, the soft part of his arm there, halfway between his elbow and his wrist.

12

The bat dropped out of his hands. Ben went down.

Mr. Brown came running in from third, Ben's dad came down from first. When Ben looked up, Robbie was there, too, looking as if he was in more pain than Ben at the moment.

Somehow Sam and Coop and Shawn were already crouched down next to Ben, Mr. Brown having to ask them to give him room.

Mr. Brown said, "Let's have a look."

Ben rolled up his sleeve. It was then that he saw the imprint of the ball's seams on the inside of his arm, like they'd been tattooed there.

Ben's dad asked Ben if he could slowly flex his arm, see if he could make a fist and bring his arm up to his shoulder, like he was doing some kind of exercise.

Ben did that.

"It hurts where I got hit," he said, "but not when I move it."

"Good," his dad said. "You probably don't want to hear this, but the only better place you could have picked is your butt."

Ben said, "Dad, I think the place I would have picked is *no* place."

13

Mr. Brown asked him to clench and unclench his left fist, then give his wrist a shake. Ben did that, too. Ben's dad gently put a thumb to Ben's arm, between the seams. "Nothing broken, not there," he said. "Would've been much worse if it got you on the elbow or wrist or hand."

Ben looked at Mr. Brown and then his dad and said, "I'm not coming out."

"Ice wouldn't be such a terrible idea," Mr. Brown said.

"What are you always saying when a guy catches one on TV?" Ben said to his dad. "Rub some dirt on it and walk it off?"

"That's what you say to the TV," Jeff McBain said, "not your son."

"I'm not gonna rub, period," Ben said.

He got up then.

He heard the applause from the bleachers, gave a quick look over there, to where his mom was standing with Lily. His arm still stung — a lot — but Ben raised it, giving them a quick wave, letting them know he was all right as he started walking up the first-base line.

Robbie Burnett walked alongside him.

"Dude," he said, "I am so sorry. If there was some way to go back and un-throw that pitch, I would."

Ben put out his fist — right fist — so Robbie could bump it and said, "Hey, I'm just glad that's all the fastball you've got."

Robbie walked back to the mound. When Ben was standing on the bag at first base his dad asked him again if he was all right and Ben said, "I'm fine, Dad, unless I need to do something left-handed on my way around the bases."

He rolled his sleeve back down so he wasn't tempted to look at the seams. Ben thinking he was going to feel a whole lot better once he scored the tying run before Darrelle or Sam scored the winning run.

Now Jeff McBain told Ben the stuff he'd been telling him all game long when he got to first base, about running hard on a ground ball, playing it halfway on a fly ball, being ready if Mr. Brown gave him the steal sign. Told him to pick up Mr. Brown as he came around second if Darrelle got a base hit to right. Told him not to take any chances on a single to left, even if the ball was in front of him.

"Can't make the first out of the inning at third," his dad said.

"Duh," Ben said.

Robbie was pitching from the stretch, keeping Ben close, not wanting him to steal. But he seemed so preoccupied with Ben that he walked Darrelle on four pitches.

First and second, nobody out, Sam up.

Sam's dad made Sam take a pitch, had to, Robbie still hadn't thrown a strike. But now he poured in strike one. Missed high with the next pitch. One and one. The third pitch was a fastball on the inside part of the base, but you couldn't beat Sam inside, his bat was too quick, he lined a ball hard between short and third, Ben having to slow down to make sure the ball didn't hit him. Thought about trying to score, but saw Mr. Brown holding him up, Ben turning to see how close to the infield their left fielder had picked up the ball.

It was the right play. Still nobody out. Justin coming to the plate.

Ben's arm wasn't hurting as much now. He knew it was this kind of moment making him feel better, the baseball fan in him loving this. Their power hitter against the other team's power pitcher, strength on strength, game on the line.

"On the ground, you gotta bust it home," Mr. Brown said.

Ben nodded, thinking that a ball on the ground would be some sort of major upset now, with Justin's smooth uppercut swing. Worst case, as long as Justin didn't strike out again? A sac fly to tie the game.

Best case?

A walk-off grand slam to start the season.

Ben watched Mr. Brown run through his signals, touching his cap first, telling Justin to swing away at the first good pitch he saw.

But Justin didn't do that, took a fastball right down the middle, watching the ball slap into the catcher's mitt. Shook his head, asked for time, like he had to regroup after taking a pitch that good. Adjusted his batting gloves, got back in. Took his stance.

Swung at the next pitch, one up in his eyes, missing it by a foot.

0-2.

"Just takes one, Jus," Ben calling out from third, forgetting about his arm in the moment, clapping his hands, just doing that sending a jolt up his arm.

The next pitch was as good as strike one had been. What Coop liked to call a "crush-me fastball." Waist high. Right down Main Street.

Justin didn't miss this one. But he didn't do much with it, either. Barely got a piece of it, hitting a one-hopper right back to Robbie. Ben wasn't even halfway to the plate when Robbie threw to the catcher for the force, the catcher then firing the ball to first to double up Justin Bard.

Two outs, just like that. Ben knew: You didn't see a lot of double plays at their age level, and you hardly ever saw one as easy as that, Darrelle on third now, Sam on second. Still a chance to win if Shawn could get a hit.

Shawn jumped on a 1-1 pitch, hitting a shot high to left-center, everybody on the bench jumping up as they watched the flight of the ball, Coop yelling "Get out!" from the on-deck circle, all of them thinking — hoping — that Shawn had gotten all of it.

Shawn knew better.

He'd tell them that he knew he'd just missed it, knew he'd just caught it an inch too close to the end of his fancy new Easton bat, watched along with everybody else as Parkerville's center fielder ran the ball down six feet short of the fence.

Ball game.

Ben stood in front of the Rams' bench, watched the center fielder sprint toward the infield, toward the crowd around Robbie behind the pitcher's mound, holding the ball high over his head like it was some kind of trophy.

Lot of firsts tonight, he thought as he went to get the ice pack in Mr. Brown's first aid kit.

First game, first loss.

First time he'd ever been hit by a pitch in his life.

Mr. Brown did the same thing he did after every practice and every game, had the whole team go sit in a circle around him in the outfield grass behind first base.

When the players settled in around him tonight, he said, "Well, an awful lot happened in that last inning, didn't it?"

"None of it good," Coop said. "I'm just sayin'."

"And I'm saying you're wrong, Coop," Mr. Brown said.

Sam made a gasping sound and said, "Impossible!"

The guys laughed. So did Sam's dad.

"Seriously," his dad said. "We loaded the bases against one of the hardest throwers in the league and had our cleanup guy at the plate. I'll take that exact same situation in every single game we play the rest of the season. Robbie just made a great pitch on Justin, is all. That's just baseball. I know you guys hear this from me all the time. But the other team wants to win, too."

Ben sat there between Sam and Coop, holding the ice to the inside of his arm, knowing Mr. Brown was right. Two teams, one winner, that's the way it always worked, no crying about it afterward, like the guy said in that movie about women playing baseball, *A League of Their Own*, no crying in baseball.

And this wasn't football, or even basketball, you didn't have to wait a week to play your next game, they had Darby coming on, right here at Highland Park, a few nights later.

From behind him he heard Justin say, "You can try to make me feel better all you want. But I would have been better off getting hit the way Ben did, we would've won the game."

Ben turned around, grinning, offered him the ice pack, and said, "Okay, you need to put this on your *head*."

"I'm not kidding."

"No," Ben said. "You're *crazy*. If we played them again right now, I'd still want you up there in that situation."

In a voice way too small for a guy as big as Justin, he said, "I know you're trying to be a good teammate, McBain. It's what you do. But everybody sitting here knows I cost us the game."

Ben noticed now how red his eyes were, afraid in that moment that there might be some crying in baseball, from Justin. A guy who was usually as happy and upbeat on a baseball field as Cooper Manley was.

Before anybody on the Rams could say anything else Justin said, "Coach, can I leave a little early today? My mom's here."

Usually Justin's mom and dad both came to games, Justin's dad had been a big baseball star at the University of Connecticut when he was young, had been drafted by the

Orioles, but never made it out of the minor leagues before he started his own company. Ben had asked Justin one time what kind of company his dad owned and he said, "The kind that buys up other companies."

"Go ahead, big man," Mr. Brown said. "Just remember: We had our chances all night long to score more runs and didn't. It's never just one player who loses a game."

"Tonight it was," Justin said, got up, walked slowly toward the parking lot, bat over his shoulder, first baseman's mitt in his hand. Head down. Like they'd lost the last game of the season and not the first.

Mr. Brown watched him go and when Justin was out of ear-shot he said, "That's just one more guy on our team who wants to win in the worst way. See you all at practice tomorrow."

When they were all up Mr. Brown said to Ben, "How you feeling?"

Ben said, "Better than Justin."

They had snacks even after night games, Darrelle's mother having brought bottles of Gatorade and water, bags of chips, and her own homemade chocolate-chip cookies. Ben, Sam, Coop, and Shawn got their cookies and drinks and went and sat in the bleachers.

"Justin wouldn't feel nearly as lousy if I'd done my job," Shawn said.

"But that's the thing," Ben said, "you *did* do your job: You hit the snot out of the ball. Guy just ran it down this time."

Coop said to Ben, "Take the ice off for a second so I can see your arm. Sam said you could see the seams of the ball."

Ben showed him. "Wow," Coop said. "I can almost see 'Rawlings,' too."

"Thanks for sharing," Ben said.

"No, listen, I think it's cool," Coop said. "Like a badge of honor." His face brightened, the way it did when what he considered a brilliant thought came to him. "What's that book we had to read that I had so much trouble getting through?"

"I'm afraid you'll have to be a little more specific," Sam said.

Ben knew. "*The Red Badge of Courage*," he said.

"Exactly!" Coop said. He pointed at Ben's arm now, if not red then certainly pink from the ice and the seams. "Red Badge of Courage McBain!"

But Ben didn't feel brave.

Just tired and sore and ready to go home. Mr. Brown was right. A lot had happened in that last inning. And Coop had been right, too. None of it good, whether they'd loaded the bases or not.

Ben always went back to a line his dad liked to use, one that the old football coach Bill Parcells had said one time:

In the end, nobody remembered why you lost.

Just that you lost.

Ben was up in his room, on his bed, watching the Yankees play an interleague game against the San Francisco Giants on his laptop, his dad once again having purchased a season ticket on MLB.TV so both he and Ben could watch any game they wanted to on their laptops. There weren't all that many shortstops right now that he wanted to watch, but he still liked watching Derek Jeter, even though Jeter was old. And he loved watching Brandon Crawford of the Giants, who could not only catch everything, but had one of the strongest arms on an infielder Ben had ever seen.

There was a knock on his door, his dad poked his head in.

"No more ice?" Jeff McBain said.

"My arm was starting to feel like a Popsicle without a stick."

His dad sat down on the end of the bed.

"That was not a boring game," he said.

"You think?" Ben said.

"I can't ever remember you getting hit before."

"I never did. I still can't believe I couldn't get out of the way."

His dad pointed at Ben's laptop. "Happens to those guys all the time."

"The pitchers are throwing ninety," Ben said. "Or more."

"Robbie was a lot closer than they are in the big leagues," his dad said. "And as hard as he throws, it probably looked like it was coming at you a hundred miles an hour."

Ben grinned. "Dad," he said, "I'm good, I really am. I've been hit way harder in football than that ball hit me tonight."

He muted the sound on the game. Sometimes he could just tell when his dad was settled in, wanted to talk. This was one of those times.

"I know you're good," Jeff McBain said.

"You want to know something funny? Right before our first practice, I was saying to the guys that all I wanted was for nothing bad to happen this season. Like Sam getting hurt in basketball because I made him stay out and practice with me that night."

There was a small park right next to their house that Ben and his friends called McBain Field. There was enough room for them to play touch football, a basketball halfcourt at the far end, next to one swing set. Ben had played a lot of ball out there in his life, so had the rest of the Core Four, even before Shawn came along. But it wasn't the best court, and Sam had stepped in a hole and missed the rest of the season, except for that last game against Darby.

Ben still blamed himself.

"The good news is that it wasn't all that bad," his dad said.

"Easy for you to say," Ben said, smiling at his dad. "That thing felt like a rock."

"Tell me about it! I took one off my knee one year when I was about your age and that knee was still sore when football started up."

"You never told me about that."

"Not one of my choicer sports memories," his dad said. "I prefer the ones that don't hurt."

"I'll be ready for practice tomorrow."

"Let's at least wait and see how it feels when you wake up in the morning."

"You want me to high-five you, show you it's better already?"

"I already know how tough you are, big boy."

His dad got up, kissed him on the top of the head, closed the door behind him as he left. Ben went back to his game. Jeter batting against Tim Lincecum. Jeter holding out his right hand to the home plate ump, his way of saying he wasn't quite ready to hit. Taking his stance. *His* bat held high. Ready now. Lincecum went into his windup, came inside with a fast-ball. Way inside. Jeter didn't bail out, didn't even move his feet or leave the batter's box, just threw his butt and his hips back even though the ball nearly grazed his belt buckle.

According to the little box in the top corner of the screen, the pitch had come in at ninety-four miles an hour.

Jeter showed the ball no respect, no fear.

No other way to be.

Ben knew you couldn't be afraid and hit a baseball, he had seen plenty of guys in Little League whose knees started to buckle as soon as the ball left the pitcher's hand. Or who didn't step toward the pitcher with their front foot, instead stepped into what was known as the "bucket," stepped toward third base if they were a right-handed hitter or first if they hit lefty.

On the laptop screen, Jeter went into his routine again, took his stance, lined the next pitch he saw from Lincecum right back up the middle so hard it was like he was trying to cut Lincecum's hair with the ball.

Out of curiosity, Ben went to a Derek Jeter stats page on the Internet and found he had been hit by pitches more than 160 times in his career.

It was part of the game, even for the most famous players in the world. How had Coop put it on the way home tonight? He had called it the "price of doing business."

Ben watched the rest of the inning, shut off his laptop. Shut the lights. Enough baseball for one night.

Closed his eyes and wondered what it was like for the great Derek Jeter the first time he couldn't get out of the way.

The next day his arm still hurt enough when Ben tried to grip a bat that both Mr. Brown and his dad decided to have him skip batting practice.

"We'll give it one more day," Mr. Brown said. "One thing about you, you're not going to forget how to hit."

"Plus," Ben said, "now I've discovered how to *get* hit."

"Well," his dad said, "I don't think you actually discovered it."

Ben had wanted to take some cuts today, just to get back at it, see how he did the day after, standing in there against Mr. Brown, who loved to pitch BP to them. And who could really throw. And who gave them no breaks on the way he came at them. The only thing he'd do, just to make it more of a fair fight, was stand about ten feet behind the pitcher's mound. But then he'd throw as hard as he could, his theory being simple enough: If you could get around on his fastball, you could do that with any eleven- or twelve-year-old fastball in the Butler County League.

But on this day, Ben's batting practice consisted of standing out at shortstop — for some reason the ball landing in the pocket of his glove didn't bother him — or making his way around the bases while the other guys hit, some of them trash-talking Mr. Brown, Coop nailing one over Shawn's head in the outfield one time and asking if Mr. Brown's arm was bothering him.

Mr. Brown yelled back at him, "Now remember, Coop, if the ball manages to slip and you get buzzed, it's considered bad form to rush the pitcher's mound when your coach is doing the pitching."

Coop said, "I thought you taught us to not only rush the mound, but bring our bat with us."

"Joking," Mr. Brown said.

"Oh," Darrelle said from the on-deck circle, "you mean I wasn't supposed to tell my mom you said that?"

All of them having fun today.

All except Justin. From the time he'd gotten to Highland Park, he acted as if last night's game had just ended, as if he'd just hit into that double play. When it was his turn in the box, he acted as if he wanted to hit every pitch he was seeing from Mr. Brown out of Rockwell, and maybe halfway to the moon.

He finally connected a couple of times, nothing over the fence, coming close one time before Sam made an over-the-shoulder catch in center. But the rest of the time it was weak pop-ups, two slow rollers to Ben at short, and a bunch of pitches he missed by a foot.

Like he was the one who had forgotten how to hit.

When practice was over and they were sitting in the outfield grass, Mr. Brown talked mostly about the Darby game on Friday night.

"I've got this crazy feeling," Mr. Brown said, "that we don't want to fall to oh-and-two, and we certainly don't want to do that against the Darby Bears."

"I'd rather go to summer school than lose to Darby," Coop said.

"Wow," Darrelle said.

"I mean it," Coop said.

"No," Darrelle said, "I meant, wow, I just assumed you *were* in summer school."

They all laughed, came together and put their hands in the middle of the circle, yelled "Beat Darby!" and started walking toward the parking lot where their parents were waiting for them.

Ben jogged to catch up with Justin.

"Hey," he said.

"Hey," Justin said. "How's your arm? I should've asked."

"I'll live," Ben said.

They kept walking.

Ben said, "How are *you* feeling?"

"What's that mean?"

The words came out of him too fast and too loud.

"Whoa," Ben said. "You just seemed real upset last night, and you don't seem much better today."

"I lost the game for us," Justin said, "in case you already forgot."

Still loud.

"C'mon, man, you know better than that. This isn't golf or tennis. Or even boxing. It wasn't you playing Parkerville all by yourself. We all lost."

"*We* didn't mess up an easy ground ball," Justin said. "And *we* didn't totally mess up a rally that was about to win us the game."

Ben said, "You are going to win us so many games this season it'll be stupid."

"You know what's stupid right now?" Justin said. Eyes starting to get red again. "Everything."

Ben realized he had left his glove on the bench. Told Justin to hang in there, he'd see him tomorrow. Saw Justin's mom waving from the passenger side of what must have been a new black SUV for them. Watched as the car pulled away. Ben thinking it was as much like a black cloud leaving as a black car.

Sam said, "He okay?"

"Not even close."

"But you're gonna try to help him."

"Yeah."

"Shocker."

"He's a teammate," Ben said, "and a friend."

Sam smiled.

"Not like you," he said. "Not like you."

Ben texted Lily after dinner, still early in the night, not close to being dark yet, asked if she wanted to come over to McBain Field and hang out.

The answer was pure Lily and came right back at him, just because nobody could text faster than Lily Wyatt.

As opposed to coming over and NOT hanging out, McBain?

Ben was going to hit her with an LOL, but they both thought LOL was dumber than choir practice, and so he just told her to get moving.

Truth was, he didn't just want to hang out, go out and sit on those swings, something they'd been doing their whole lives, from the time they were sitting on their moms' laps. Now it was just the two of them, talking about anything and everything. And they might end up doing that later tonight, just because Ben *did* love it when it was just him and Lily. Listening to her. Hearing her laugh. Trying to keep up with a brain traveling faster than the speed of sound. Allowing her inside his own brain — sometimes without permission — and into his heart, just because nobody knew him the way she did.

Before they talked tonight, though, he wanted her to pitch to him.

It wasn't going to be regulation hardballs, just some old beat-up tennis balls. Ben didn't care. He wanted to hit. His grip on the bat wasn't much better than it had been at practice.

He still wanted to hit on the night after he'd gotten hit.

Sam had asked after practice if Justin was okay. Ben just wanted to make sure he was. It wasn't something he wanted to talk about with the guys, with Sam or Coop or Shawn. Or even his dad. He didn't want them to start thinking this was an issue with him. A *thing*.

Him and the ball.

Lily was different. He'd always been able to talk about stuff with Lily, share stuff with Lily, that he didn't with anybody else. She liked to tell everybody that she was one of the boys. But she really wasn't.

When she got to McBain, she'd brought her glove with her. Like somehow she knew things already.

"Figured you might want to throw the ball around," she said, "test out that wounded wing."

"Wounded wing?"

"I just liked the sound of it."

Ben said, "Actually, I want you to pitch to me."

Lily threw a low uppercut into the air and said, *"Yes!"*

Then she started windmilling her arm. "You know I can pitch as well as any *guy*," she said.

Making "guy" sound like something that would crawl out from under a rock.

"I know, Lils," Ben said. "Boy oh boy, do I know."

He ran to the garage and got a bucket of tennis balls, came back to the field with the balls and his bat, went back to the garage and got his old pitch-back net so they wouldn't have to chase balls if he swung and missed.

Not that he was planning to do much of that.

"*Tennis* balls?" she said. "Really?"

"Hardballs break windows," Ben said, "maybe you hadn't heard."

Lily shrugged. "Only if you hit them," she said, walked off the forty-six feet — she knew that the way she knew just about everything else — that was the distance between the pitcher's mound and home plate.

"This is *so* on," she said.

"Can't this just be fun," Ben said, "since they wouldn't let me hit this afternoon?"

Lily smiled. A great, big Lily smile. "Of *course*," she said. "But can I ask one question?"

"What?"

"Don't you want to wear a helmet?"

He took some practice swings, felt it a little in his arm, not like before. Or so he told himself.

"You good?" Lily said.

"Never better," Ben said.

He took a couple of pitches that weren't close to being strikes, Lily saying she wasn't warmed up yet. Swung and missed. Fouled one back. Then tagged one over her head in the direction of the basketball court at McBain, the swings.

It was after a dozen pitches that Lily put up a hand and said, "Stop flinching."

Ben said, "I'm not flinching."

"Yes," she said, "you are."

Smiling as she said it, but making it sound like the most obvious thing in the world.

"You're being ridiculous," Ben said. "I just hit one to the swings. I think the ball is still rolling."

"You're hitting tennis balls against *me*, McBain," Lily said, "not against one of your boys from All-Stars."

"You know you've got an arm," Ben said. "And you know you live to get me to swing and miss."

"Well, that part is true," Lily said. "But I hear you guys talking sometimes about how somebody has a hitch in their swing. I'm just seeing a little hitch in *you*, especially if the ball is anywhere near you."

"If you think you're being funny, you're not."

Ben felt himself getting agitated, hearing it in his own voice, knowing that was never a good thing with Lily Wyatt.

Now she put her hands on her hips. Never a good sign.

"I'm not trying to be funny, if I was trying to be funny, you'd be laughing," she said. "I'm just trying to tell you something."

"Something wrong."

"So I'm lying?"

"I didn't say that, Lils. I said you were wrong."

"Because I don't agree with you on this, I'm wrong?"

"I didn't say that, either."

He knew he should get out of this now, try to find a way to stop it before it got any worse, but before he could Lily said, "This is why you wanted me to come over here, isn't it?"

Seeing right into him again.

Ben waited.

"You wanted to find out if you're afraid of the ball," she said. "Any ball. And now because I think you might be, even if it's just a little bit, you're getting mad at me."

"I'm not mad at you," he said. "I just wanted to get some swings, is all."

"Do you want me to tell you what I really think?"

"Do I have a choice?"

Lily let that one go. "Your swing is fine," she said. "It's just that your front leg is buckling a little bit, which maybe only I'd notice, because I notice pretty much everything with you. And a few times, when the ball did come near you, you looked like you were stepping toward Mrs. Palmer's house."

Across the street. Like it was on the third-base side of his neighborhood.

"Maybe I did," Ben said, wanting this to be over. "You're probably right."

"Don't tell me I'm right when you don't think I'm right."

Ben said, "So I'm wrong if I think you're wrong, and I'm wrong when I think you're right?"

"You don't think I'm right, but I am."

"You know what I don't want to do? Argue with you."

"Too late," she said. "Next time I will just lie to you."

Ben dropped his bat, put up his hands now, like he was Mr. Brown holding up a runner who thought he could score.

"For the last time," Ben said, "I wasn't calling you a liar, I'd never call you that."

"Okay," she said.

"Okay for real?" Ben said. "Or are you just saying that because you want to stop talking about this?"

"Little bit of both."

"You want to come in and watch TV?"

She shook her head. "I think I'll head home," she said. "You want me to help you pick up balls before I do?"

"I got 'em," Ben said. "And, Lils? Thanks for coming over."

"You're welcome," she said. "I think."

She went over, hooked her glove over the handlebar of her bike, pedaled slowly across the grass toward the street. Stopped, put a leg out to steady herself, looked over her shoulder.

"This isn't a big deal, Big Ben," she said. "And I'm sure you'll be fine when you get back with the guys tomorrow." She shrugged and smiled. "But maybe the one lying to you tonight was *you*."

Before he could answer she took off up the street, Ben watching her go, watching her pick up speed until she made the turn on Stone Street and disappeared, feeling himself getting angry all over again.

Mostly because she was right.

Ben caught a break at batting practice the next day, Mr. Brown not there because of business, Sam pitching when it was Ben's turn to lead them off.

And when Sam, or Shawn, or even Coop pitched BP, they all had just one purpose:

Lay the ball in there so their teammates could hit it very, very hard someplace.

Ben was glad he was hitting right away, just wanting to get a helmet on, get a bat in his hands. Get on with it. Or get it over with, because that's the way he was really feeling today. Most days he couldn't wait to get to practice and take his cuts.

But he knew this wasn't most days.

His arm was still sore. Amazingly, you could still see the seams, even though the outline was getting fainter now. He knew he could have begged out for another day, waited until the Darby game to get back in the box. Only that wasn't him. To him that would have practically been like faking an injury, even though the injury he'd suffered the other night was legit.

Definitely not him, whether he was feeling like himself today or not.

He had been telling himself since he went to sleep last night that he wasn't going to flinch. One of his dad's favorite expressions was "standing in there against the curve," he was always telling Ben that you had to stand in there against the curve, and not just in baseball. Ben knew he wasn't going to see any curveballs today, Mr. Brown didn't allow his pitchers to throw them even in batting practice. He wasn't even going to see any fastballs from Sam, just a hitter's favorite thing in the world:

Straight balls.

"Go easy on me," he said to Sam from the batter's box. "I was viciously attacked by Robbie Burnett the other night."

"We thought you got hit on purpose because you knew you couldn't catch up with Robbie's heat," Sam said.

"Oh, I see," Ben said. "I let the heat catch up with *me*."

"Pretty much."

"Shut up and pitch."

"I can do that," Sam said, grinning, went into a big showy windup with a lot of leg kick, like he was going to come with his own high heat.

Then pushed one up there that was like the overhand version of slow-pitch softball.

Ben felt himself stepping toward third instead of right at Sam, he couldn't help himself. But he still managed to time the pitch and line it over Darrelle's head at third base and into left field.

"He's baaaaack," Darrelle said.

Ben knew better than that. But at least he was back in there, feeling like he'd gotten up after getting knocked down. That was really who he was, he knew that about himself. That was the athlete he'd always tried to be. When he got knocked down driving hard to the hoop in basketball, he made sure to go right back at the same guy, first chance he got. Not in a cocky way. Just his way of saying, *That all you got?* Same in football, especially now that he was playing quarterback. If he got put down hard, either standing in the pocket or scrambling, he made sure to bounce right back up before the guy who tackled him did, sometimes waiting to pat the guy on the back, letting him know it was all good, despite the fact that Ben was usually the smallest guy in the game.

This was different, because being a hitter in baseball was different, it wasn't just one pitch or one swing that put you in the clear. Cleared your head.

You had to keep standing in there.

He got five more swings before he laid down a bunt. Two were ground balls to short. One a fly ball to short center. Finally there was a flare to right field that would have been a hit in a game. Ben felt like he opened up way too soon on that one, his left hip feeling like a screen door flying open in the wind. But his hands were good enough and his batter's eye was good enough for him to put the bat on the ball.

Then he dropped a perfect bunt down the third-base line, nobody on their team being a better bunter than he was, the joke with the rest of the guys being that Ben could get a bunt down even if the pitcher tried to throw behind him, he was that good with the bat.

Done.

Ben took off his helmet, went over and placed it with the rest, laid his bat down in the grass, got his glove, ran out to shortstop. His heart still beating fast and hard, the way it did before a big at bat in a game. Ben feeling that way today in practice.

Usually there was nobody on the field who loved swinging a baseball bat more than he did. Today he just loved that he was done.

"Smoked that one over my head," Darrelle said from third.

"Sam couldn't have made it easier if he'd placed the ball on a tee," Ben said. "If I can't hit that slop, I should find another sport."

"I'm right here," Sam said from the mound.

"How's the arm today?" Darrelle said to Ben.

"Better."

But Ben knew that his arm wasn't the problem right now, his head was.

It figured that Chase Braggs would be the starting pitcher for Darby, it just did.

Chase Braggs: Ben's nemesis from the basketball season, the full-of-himself star for the Darby Bears.

You couldn't make this stuff up, as Coop liked to say.

Chase had moved to Darby at the start of the last school

year, turned out to be a total star in basketball, and knew it. It was why Ben and the guys had decided, after playing him in just one preseason scrimmage, that his last name was really a verb:

Chase *Braggs*.

It turned out that what Chase mostly wanted to do, after hearing so much from other kids in Darby about all the things Ben McBain could do in sports, was prove that he wasn't just a bigger version of Ben in basketball, that he was better.

Which he did for most of the season. He wanted to beat Ben in basketball, he wanted to steal the spotlight from him, he even wanted to steal Lily away from Ben once the game was over. That was why the real rivalry all winter wasn't just Rockwell vs. Darby, it was Ben vs. Chase.

Chase got the better of it until the last game of the regular season. Ben played badly against him in their two meetings before that, and kept finding ways to act even worse when he was in the same place with Chase and Lily.

Darby would end up winning the league. But they didn't go undefeated because Sam came back from his sprained ankle and Ben played the best he had all year, finishing it off by making the game-winning shot over Chase. The game that felt like a championship game but really wasn't.

Ben and Chase finally made peace when the game was over, Chase even admitting that he thought the Rams were better when they had Sam on the court. It didn't exactly make Ben and Chase *boys*. It was probably a stretch to say that they were friends now.

They respected each other enough to get along, put it that way. Chase had backed off — permanently — from Lily, figuring out that just being good at basketball, or even great, wasn't ever going to change the friendship that Ben and Lily had. But Ben and Chase Braggs both knew they were going to be competing — hard — against each other for a long time, maybe all the way through high school, and that they should try to focus on that, without any hard feelings.

Starting with tonight's game, the first time they'd met up since Ben made that shot over Chase in basketball.

"Heard Robbie Burnett thought your elbow was part of the strike zone," Chase said when he came over to say hello to Ben and Sam and Coop and Shawn before the game, right before Darby took the field for infield practice.

"Good thing it *wasn't* my elbow," Ben said, "or I would have spent the summer in a cast. Or at least a sling."

"Well, don't worry about tonight," Chase said. "Even though I have a better fastball than Robbie, I have much better control."

Ben grinned, couldn't help it, nice to know that Chase hadn't stopped being Chase.

"How do you know what kind of fastball Robbie has?" Ben said. "You haven't even faced him yet."

Chase shrugged. "Nobody in this league could possibly have a better fastball than I do."

"Are you saying that you're better at baseball than basket-ball?" Ben said.

Chase reached out so they could all pound him some fist before he walked away.

"You guys decide after I shut you down and shut you out tonight," he said, then turned and jogged across the infield to the Darby bench on the third-base side of Highland Park.

Sam said, "You're *sure* we like that guy now?"

"We like him better," Ben said.

"Maybe we should just say that we don't hate him," Coop said, "and leave it at that."

"C'mon," Ben said, "you know he's just trying to be funny."

Coop's face was blank as he said, "Ha. Ha. Ha."

Ben said, "Think of him as what my mom likes to call a work in progress."

"Lot of work," Shawn said.

"Whole lot," Sam said.

Then he turned to Ben and said, "Are we going to let him shut us down tonight?"

Ben smiled and shook his head slowly from side to side, wanting to feel as confident as he knew Sam was, even though he didn't know what to expect the first time he had to face Chase Braggs, face real pitching for the first time since the Parkerville game.

"Didn't think so," Sam Brown said.

Sam was pitching the first three innings against Darby tonight, Shawn was pitching the next two, Mr. Brown had told Ben he wanted him to be his closer tonight in the sixth.

Before the Rams took infield, Mr. Brown had said, "The arm's ready, right?"

"Both of them," Ben had said.

*   *   *

Sam struck out the side in the top of the first, finally blowing a fastball of his own right past Chase to end the inning. From shortstop it looked to Ben as if the pitch was coming in at the knees but then just seemed to explode when it got to home plate and ended up being what the announcers like to call "belt-high cheese," Chase having no chance against it, like Sam had slam-dunked on him.

When they got to the bench Ben said, "You think Chase wants to revise his fastball rankings for the Butler County League?"

"Let's see what he's got," Sam said. "If he can pitch as well as he chirps."

Their word for trash talk.

"You really love his chirp, don't you?" Ben said.

"Yeah," Sam said, "like I love eating vegetables."

Ben walked to the plate then, telling himself the same thing he'd been telling himself all day: That he loved to hit, that he'd always been a good hitter, that one pitch wasn't going to change that, come on.

And telling himself something else: That no matter how Chase had been bragging on his fastball, it was hard to believe that anybody he was going to face this summer could throw a fastball harder than Robbie Burnett.

Which meant: That the worst thing that was going to happen to him this season had already happened.

He walked around behind the ump, said hello to Ryan Hurley, the Darby catcher, somebody they'd played against in football and basketball. Dug in with his back foot. Like always. Put out his right hand to the ump as he did. Like Jeter. Then set his hands, high.

Whole new ball game, in all ways.

Took a ball, high. Willing to keep his front foot locked in place.

Chase decided to mess with him with his next pitch, maybe because he couldn't help himself, maybe because he was always going to be looking for an edge with Ben. So he dropped down low and threw sidearm, came with this sweeping arm motion like he was trying to reach out and touch the Darby bench.

And came inside on Ben.

Way inside.

Ben fell back to get out of the way, didn't fall down, just avoided the pitch like he was dodging a ball in a recess game of dodge ball. Heard the ump say it was ball two. Stood where he was, just for a beat longer than he needed to, so he could give Chase a long look. Sam would tell him when he got back to the bench that Chase was smiling after he threw the ball, like he enjoyed the sight of Ben bailing out.

But all Chase did now was hold up a hand and say, "Sorry, dude. Haven't mastered that pitch yet."

"Yeah," Ben said.

"Slipped."

"Yeah."

Saying that to the guy who'd just told him he had practically the best control on the planet.

"Let's play," the ump said.

Ben got back in there, wanting in the worst way to line one right up the middle and right through Chase Braggs. But he was way too far ahead of a fastball, taking a wild, off-balance hack at it, missing by a lot. Letting everybody see how much he wanted a hit, his whole body flinching this time.

Finally he worked the count full, then was too over-anxious again on the 3-2 pitch, hitting a slow roller to the second baseman on a ball he knew — *knew* — he would normally have jumped all over and pulled. But once again he opened up way too soon, all he could do was push the ball to the right side.

He busted it out of the box, nearly beat the play, trying to steal an infield single, out by a step.

When he got back to the bench Coop said, "Trying to go the other way?"

Ben took off his helmet, banged it on the bench, steamed.

"Yeah," he said, "with one of the ugliest swings of all time."

"You okay?" Coop said, staring at him. "It's only the bottom of the first."

"I'm never okay when I make an out," Ben said. "Okay?"

"I think this anger is something we can use," Coop said, and Ben couldn't help himself, he laughed.

"You really are an idiot," Ben said.

Coop said, "But much, *much* funnier than Chase Braggs."

Sam only gave up one hit and one walk in his three innings, struck out six guys. Chase gave up a double to Sam in the first, then pretty much shut the Rams down from there, walking two guys, one of them Ben in the third, Ben barely checking his swing on a 3-2 pitch in the dirt.

The game was still scoreless in the bottom of the fourth when Justin Bard got tossed from the game.

Sam had just tripled to lead off the bottom of the fourth against Chase's replacement, a ball between the center fielder and left fielder that should have only been a double, would have been a double for just about anybody in the game except Sam Brown even though it didn't roll all the way to the wall.

Ben had always thought his friend didn't just run *like* the wind, he was faster than that. So he wasn't surprised when Sam busted it out of the box the way he did, the action in front of him all the way, somehow running as if he knew the whole time that he could make third, cutting the bag at second perfectly, the bag almost propelling him toward third, beating the cut-off throw from the shortstop standing up. Not even breathing hard. Smiling over at Ben, maybe just because of the pure fun of being able to run the bases like that.

Or just being Sam, knowing he had that extra gear in him whenever he needed it.

"Anything better than watching Sam leg out a triple?" Coop said on the bench.

"How about a knock from Justin to score him?" Ben said.

"Doesn't have to be a knock," Coop said. "I'll take an RBI even if we have to give up an out. Bet he will, too."

Justin had had what Coop called a "glorious" oh-fer to start the season against Parkerville. Then he'd taken a called third strike against Chase to start tonight's game. This after missing yesterday's practice, one of the guys saying he had something he had to do with his parents.

Ben had been watching him closely during batting practice, saw that Justin didn't even hit one ball hard then.

He's hitting worse than me right now, Ben thought, and he didn't even *get* hit.

Ben didn't know the kid pitching for Darby, just could see that he wasn't as big as Chase, didn't have nearly as much velocity. He was a strike thrower, though, always a good thing in baseball. Mr. Brown was always telling his pitchers, "There may be better things for a pitcher than strike one and strike two, but nobody's discovered them in about a hundred and fifty years."

He threw strike one to Justin now, inside corner. Justin turned and gave the ump a quick look. Ump just nodded at him. Ben knew the ump was right. Maybe not the most hittable pitch ever thrown. But a strike. Mostly because that's the way it had just been called.

Lot of chatter from the Rockwell bench now. And from Sam at third. All the usual baseball chatter that always made Sam smile, just because it was something else that probably hadn't changed in about a hundred and fifty years in baseball. Just takes one. Be a batter. Wait for your pitch. You got this guy.

Justin Bard had heard it all before because they all had, from the time they first started playing T-ball.

The kids on the Darby bench and the Darby infielders were chattering away themselves. Go after this guy. Throw strikes. *You* got this.

Like they'd all made selections from the same baseball iTunes list.

Justin swung right through strike two, taking a huge rip, nearly losing his helmet, almost as if he were trying to make up for the bad swings he'd made in the first two games with just one good one.

0-and-2.

Ben stared at Justin, wondering what was in *his* head right now, wondering what thoughts were getting in *his* way. Wondering why somebody this good was pressing this much so early in the season. Squeezing the bat this hard. A few at bats to start the season, that was all it was. A few at bats to start the *summer.* He was doing what they were all doing, playing summer ball with his boys and Ben was trying to understand — he was always trying to understand sports, like sports was his favorite subject in school — why Justin Bard, who had the best swing on their team, was this messed up.

The pitcher had to know he had him now, had to be seeing what they were all seeing, that Justin was ready to get himself out again, and wasn't going to need a whole lot of help.

The pitcher decided to make him chase, threw a ball that bounced nearly a foot in front of home plate. Didn't matter.

Justin took another wild swing. Ryan Hurley, the Darby catcher, had to make a nice play boxing the ball, keeping it in front of him, keeping Sam at third, jumping up and tagging Justin out, Justin not even running even though the ball had been in the dirt.

As soon as Ryan did tag him, and started running the ball back to the pitcher, that was when Justin flung his bat down the first-base line in disgust. Or anger. Or embarrassment.

Maybe all of the above.

Nobody saw it coming, Ben couldn't remember him ever having done that before. Nothing anybody could have done to stop it. It just happened. That fast. Maybe not everybody else on the bench knew what that meant, but Ben McBain did, he knew the rules as well as the coaches did, knew exactly what was going to happen next.

The umpire stepped out from behind the plate, made the motion that meant he was calling time, took off his mask, pointed at Justin, and then pointed in the direction of the Rams' bench. He could have been pointing to the parking lot, or downtown Rockwell, because Justin Bard had just been ejected.

"Son," the ump said, "you're out of the game."

Justin put his head down, started walking toward the bench. Ben was already halfway to the field, going to get Justin's bat for him. But the ump said to Ben, "Leave it where it is." To Justin he said, "You go get your own bat. *Then* take a seat for the rest of the night."

Justin made a slight left turn, having to know that every-body in Highland Park, both teams, the fans, *everybody*, were looking at him in that moment. Just not the way he ever would have wanted.

He stopped just long enough to turn back to the ump and say, "It was an accident."

"Doesn't matter."

"I've never thrown a bat before!" Justin said, probably louder than he intended, sounding a little bit like you did when your parents caught you doing something you knew you shouldn't have been doing.

"And I expect you won't ever do it again," the ump said in a quiet voice. "Now please go collect that bat so we can resume the game."

A game that would go on without Justin now. The way the next game the Rams played would go on without him, Ben not sure that Justin had even processed *that* yet. Another rule of the Butler County League, for any sport they played: If you got tossed from a game, no matter what the reason, you were automatically suspended from the next game, too.

Justin leaned down, picked up his bat, took what must have felt like the longest walk he'd ever taken on a ball field, placed his bat with the rest at the end of the Rams' bench, took a seat at the end closest to right field, plenty of space between him and Darrelle. It was where he was sitting, not even watching the game, when Shawn ripped a clean single to right, scoring Sam with the first run of the game.

Ben waited until Coop was up — Coop about to double-home Shawn — before he went and sat down next to Justin. But before he could say anything Justin looked up at him with red eyes and said, "Please don't talk to me."

Ben said, his voice not much more than a whisper, "I just wanted to tell you I know what it's like, I'm scuffling, too, right now."

"No," Justin said.

"I am."

"No," Justin said, "you don't know what it's like."

"But . . ."

Justin got up and walked now to the *other* end of the bench, saying, "You're still talking."

When he was gone, Sam came over from getting a drink of water, sat down next to Ben. "Sometimes being a good teammate," he said, "means letting guys figure stuff out for themselves." Grinned at Ben as he said, "Hard as that is for you to understand sometimes."

"I was just trying to help."

"Help him tonight by leaving him alone."

Max Kalfus, the Rams' right fielder, singled home Coop with two outs to make it 3–0. When Coop got back to the bench, everybody got up except Justin.

When the inning was over, Mr. Brown stopped Ben before he ran back out on the field.

"You're still a shortstop right now," Mr. Brown said. "But you're going to be a closer in a couple of innings. You good with that?"

Ben grinned. "What do you think, Coach?"

It was 3–2 by the time Ben got the ball in the bottom of the sixth. He'd come to the plate one more time, walking in the bottom of the fifth, stealing second, ending up on third when Sam hit a rocket to deep center that Jeb Arcelus caught for Darby one step in front of the wall.

Ben walked Jeb to start the sixth — dumbest thing in the world for anybody trying to get the last three outs of a one-run game — and then Jeb stole second when Darrelle, who'd moved over to short replacing Ben, couldn't come up with Coop's throw.

But two outs later Jeb was still on third base, it was still a one-run game when Chase Braggs came walking to the plate. Ben thinking that maybe he'd found the best way in the world not to worry about hitting. His or Justin's.

Be a pitcher.

Ryan Hurley, in the on-deck circle, called out to Chase.

"Take him to the hoop," he said, and Ben knew it was for his benefit as much as Chase's, because of everything that had happened between them in basketball.

Ben stepped off the mound now, rubbing up the baseball, looked out to Sam in center field. Sam nodded. Ben got back up on the mound, looked in at Coop, who pointed at Ben with his mitt. Then Coop set up inside and didn't even have to move the mitt as Ben poured in strike one, Chase taking all the way.

Or maybe wanting to see what Ben had.

There was way less chatter now with the game on the line. Now Coop set up outside. In and out. Chase was swinging now, but was lucky to get a piece, fouling the ball back to the screen, putting himself in a great big oh-two hole.

Coop set up way outside, but Ben shook him off. He didn't

want to waste a pitch, didn't want Chase to get himself out. *Ben* wanted to get him out, Ben wanted to show him something he couldn't possibly know: That Chase didn't have the best fastball in the league because Ben did.

Little guy, big arm.

If you didn't know that about Ben you didn't know anything.

He'd shown Chase two fastballs so far.

Just not his best one.

He threw it now, threw a fastball that Chase maybe couldn't hit because he couldn't see it, maybe only heard it hit the middle of Cooper Manley's catcher's mitt as loudly as the crack of a bat.

Strike three.

Rams 3, Bears 2.

Ball game.

Chase didn't toss his bat, even though he seemed to think about it. Didn't look out at Ben, either. Just took his own long walk back to the Darby bench.

Ben walked down toward Coop. No fist-pumping from him, no chest-beating, no noise. Not after just their first win of the season. Coop put the ball in Ben's glove like he was spiking it and leaned close to Ben, so only he could hear, as he said, "Should we go ask Chase if he thinks you're better in baseball than you are in basketball?"

Sam was there now, having run in from center at top speed, and he said to Ben, "That didn't stink."

Shawn had moved to first after Justin had been thrown out. He said, "That absolutely did not stink."

"No," Ben said, "it did not."

The four of them walked toward the bench together. Ben found himself looking for Justin, hoping that a win like this over Darby — and Chase Braggs — might take some of the sting out of what had happened to him.

But he was already gone.

Mr. Brown had announced at the start of the season that they were never going to practice more than twice a week, probably only once in the weeks when they had three games.

"I want this to be summer ball," he said, "not a summer job."

So there was only one practice this weekend, Sunday afternoon at five o'clock, Highland Park. Until then, the Core Four Plus One had no real plan other than having some pool time at Shawn's on Saturday afternoon and then going to see a movie. Or maybe there'd be no movie, they'd just hang out with each other, which sometimes seemed like all the plan they really needed.

Before that, though, Ben had a plan for himself.

He wanted to go over to Highland Park and spend some time in the batting cage there, the one tucked into a corner of the park closest to the woods. Wanted to dial the pitching machine up to a speed as fast as Robbie Burnett or Chase Braggs — or Ben himself — and get his swing back.

And his nerve.

"Easiest game in the world," Ben's dad had always said after Ben had a big day or night at the plate. "See ball, hit ball."

Something that had always seemed as simple as it sounded until it wasn't. Ben had decided that he wasn't going to spend the whole season worrying about hitting instead of wanting to hit, wanting to practically run to the plate when it was his turn to hit.

In football, he wanted to be the quarterback because that meant the game was in his hands, he didn't have to hope somebody else made a play, he was the one in charge of that, at least until he handed the ball off or threw it. Same in basketball, why he loved being a point guard. The game had to run through him, the ball was in his hands until he gave it to somebody else.

You couldn't pass the bat in baseball, and right now he wanted to. And he just wasn't going through the whole season feeling this way. Was. Not.

His dad had a key to the cage, so did Mr. Brown. All he had to do was ask his dad for it. And if his dad asked him why he wanted it, he'd tell him enough of the truth to get by. He wanted to get in some extra hitting. True. Felt his timing was off. Totally true.

Nine o'clock Saturday morning, his dad in the kitchen, having just come back from his long Saturday morning run, still in his Boston College maroon T-shirt and shorts and running shoes, newspaper opened in front of him, tall iced coffee next to the paper.

Looked up at Ben and said, "How can I help you?"

"Can I borrow the key to the batting cage?"

His dad smiled. "My son the perfectionist," he said. "After the second game of the season you need to practice even though this was going to be a baseball-free day?"

"Just want to work on some stuff, is all."

Trying to make it sound as normal as if he were telling his dad he was on his way over to Lily's.

"Can I ask what stuff?"

"Stuff." Ben shrugged. "Thought I missed a couple of pitches the other night I shouldn't've."

Still smiling, Jeff McBain said, "Everybody misses pitches they think they shouldn't miss. Every game. From Highland Park to Fenway Park."

"You're the one who just said I was a perfectionist," Ben said.

"A blessing," his dad said, "and a curse." Took off his reading glasses and said, "Hey, I could go with you, if you want. Your mom won't be back from the farmers' market anytime soon, which means I'm exactly where I want to be for the next hour or so."

"Where you want to be," Ben said, smiling back at him, "means you have nowhere you *need* to be."

"Exactly!" his dad said, slapping a palm on the table. "I could take a look at your swing, see if I can spot any fatal flaws."

58

"Dad," Ben said, "you know sometimes I like to figure stuff out on my own."

Jeff McBain slapped the table again and said, "You're kidding, I hadn't ever noticed that!"

"Dad? The key?"

"Drawer next to the fridge," he said. "Do *not* lose it."

Ben grabbed the key, thanked his dad, headed out the door to the garage to get his bat bag, the one he could sling over his shoulder as he rode his bike, wondering why he was afraid to tell his dad the real reason he was going over there.

Maybe because right now he was afraid, period.

He was on his bike, on his way down the driveway, when he felt his cell phone buzzing. Stuck a leg down to stop, reached in, figuring it was Sam or Coop or Lily wanting to know what time he was getting to Shawn's.

Wasn't any of them.

The name in the screen was Justin Bard's.

"Hey," Ben said.

"Hey."

"How you doin'?"

"Great," Justin said in a sarcastic voice. "Nothing better than letting your team down in one game, getting kicked out of another, and then getting suspended from the next for being a bonehead."

"Dude," Ben said, "it's over, let it go."

"You mean like I did my bat?"

There was a long pause, Ben not knowing how to respond to that. Before he had to, Justin said, "Are you doing anything right now? I thought maybe I could come over or whatever."

Ben couldn't remember another time when Justin had called and asked to come over, not one time since they'd known each other, certainly not since they started playing sports together. They were boys, for sure. Just not that kind of boys.

"I'm a little jammed up right now," Ben said. "But can I hit you back in like an hour?"

"Yeah, sure, whatever," Justin said.

"Call you in an hour," Ben said. "Okay?"

No answer.

"Okay?" Ben said again.

He realized then he was talking to himself, nothing unusual about that, he felt like he'd been doing that a lot this week. He put his bike back in motion and headed up the street toward town, and the park, thinking that he was sorry Justin Bard had his problems right now, but for the next hour he needed to work on his own.

Nobody was in the cage when Ben got to the park. Not much baseball being played anywhere at Highland Park, at least not yet. Just one dad pitching underhand to his son on one of the fields, two kids who looked to be a little younger than Ben playing catch in the outfield of the other one. Other than that, Ben didn't see anybody he recognized. And was happy about that, he wanted to be alone in the cage, alone with the ball coming at him, just him and baseball on this morning.

Hit it and stop thinking so much before you did. What did his dad always say about sports? Paralysis by analysis. That was exactly where Ben was two games into the season: Baseball actually feeling like the summer job that his coach said he *didn't* want it to be.

Ben knew how to operate the new pitching machine called The Pro, they'd all learned how during the Little League season in the spring. He opened the door to the cage, hit the power switch, set the dial to fifty-five miles per hour, the speed of a good fastball in their league if not a Robbie fastball, let the machine throw a couple of pitches to make sure he had the height right.

When he had that the way he wanted to, he filled the whole bucket with balls, ran back to where the plate was in the cage, picked up his bat, took his stance, told himself to make a nice, level swing at first, not try to kill every pitch he saw.

It took him awhile to get into a groove, find his rhythm. He popped a couple of balls straight up, topped a couple, even swung through one pitch when he did try to drive it all the way through the fence behind The Pro.

First bucket wasn't so great. The second bucket, though, was much better. There were a couple of line drives Ben drove right at The Pro, would have knocked the machine right over, he was pretty sure, if there wasn't a fiberglass shield protecting it.

"Yeah," Ben said after a line drive made a sound off the shield like a firecracker going off in there. "Now you got this."

Chatter only for himself today.

There was a third bucket, and then a fourth. He lost count. At some point he dialed the sucker up to sixty miles per hour.

See what he could do with that. Hit the first one at sixty right over the top of the shield and over the top of the machine. Best swing yet. He felt himself starting to sweat now, felt his breath coming faster into this, focused totally on the ball coming out of the slot at the front of the pitching machine.

If he'd get underneath a pitch, or get out in front of one too much, he'd concentrate harder on the next, put a good swing on the next.

Feeling no pain.

When his arms finally started to get tired, he checked his cell phone, saw that he'd been there two hours. Put the phone back in his pocket, loaded up another bucket, told himself that the next pitch he really drove would be the last one of the day. Like telling yourself you were going to drain one more outside shot when you were by yourself shooting hoops.

He'd dialed the speed up to sixty-five by then, knowing it was more speed than he was likely to see all season, just crushed the second pitch he saw, like someone had drawn a target on the shield.

He stepped out, walked up to the machine, set it back to fifty-five, raised the height just a little, changed the direction slightly, went back to the plate, picked his bat back up, did something he told himself he'd do when he got there.

Made no move to get out of the way now that he'd aimed The Pro right at the batter's box for a right-handed hitter, just let the ball hit him.

He'd planned to have it hit him in the butt, but he hadn't pushed the machine far enough to the right, and when the ball was on him, it wasn't headed for his backside, it caught him square on the left wrist.

It didn't hurt the way Robbie's pitch had, even though it had hit a bone instead of the fleshy part of his arm.

But it hurt enough.

Ben wanted to cry out in pain — again — but at that moment he heard Lily's voice in the distance, Lily on her bike, heading toward the cage, Lily calling his name and waving at him at the same time.

"Don't think you can hide from me, McBain," she said when she got to the cage. "It can't be done."

"I wasn't hiding from you," he said, "and would never try to hide from you. I'm not an idiot."

"Most of the time," she said. "And not nearly as often as most guys."

"Stop it," Ben said, "all this praise will go to my head."

"You didn't get enough baseball this week?" she said.

"How did you know I was here, by the way?"

"Your dad told me," she said, "that you were here grinding away."

"I stink at hitting right now," he said. "I was trying to un-stink."

"This is what you're like when you have one bad shooting game at basketball," she said. "You have to go off by yourself and shoot, like, a thousand shots."

She was on one side of the chain-link fence, fingers hooked through the holes. He went over and leaned against the fence, too, and forgot about his wrist.

And winced.

"What?" she said.

He knew he was caught, but tried to bluff his way out.

"What what?"

"What's wrong with your wrist?"

"I did something to it right before you got here," he said. "No biggie."

"Looked like it to me," she said. "*What* did you do to it?"

Ben lowered his voice, even though it was just the two of them, no one else around, and said, "You promise not to tell?"

"If you're asking me not to tell you know I won't tell."

Ben said, "I let the ball hit me."

Lily pulled back from the fence, came around to the door of the cage, walked right up to him, and said, "I'm sorry, I couldn't possibly have heard you right. Because what I *thought* you just said was that you let a ball hit you on purpose and now you've got a sore wrist because of that." Lily put her hands on her hips — never *ever* a good sign — and said, "Are you crazy?"

"Please don't tell Sam and Coop and Shawn," he said.

"We did the part about me not telling already, McBain. What I'm telling you is that it's taken one week of the baseball season for you to turn into a raving lunatic."

Before he could say anything Lily said, "Do you need to ice your wrist?"

"It's feeling better already."

"Sure it is."

She shook her head. "You *let* the ball hit you? I think I've got it. You didn't want to come here and hit today. You wanted to *be* hit? Brilliant, McBain. I can't believe guys aren't doing this to themselves in the big leagues."

"Can I explain?"

"*May* I explain?"

"Sorry, Miss English Teacher," he said. "May I explain?'

"I can't wait to hear this."

Ben said, "I just wanted to prove to myself that I didn't have to be afraid of getting hit again in a game."

She put her hand on his wrist, didn't squeeze hard. Just hard enough for him to say, "Ow?"

"Obviously, it worked out great for you," she said.

"You know that expression about getting back up on a horse when you fall off?" Ben said. "If you think about it, that's sort of what I was trying to do."

"I think the part of the horse we need to be talking about is that back part," Lily said.

"Very funny," Ben said.

"It's a good thing I got here," Lily said. "No kidding, McBain. You would have been better off taking one off your hard head."

"I'm fine," he said. "Really."

"Really?" she said.

His wrist was actually starting to hurt more — hurt a *lot* — but he would have been willing to take a pitch off the helmet before he was going to admit that to Lily Wyatt.

"But since you think I'm in such terrible pain, you probably want to help me pick up balls, right?"

"No," she said. "But I'm willing to watch you do it!"

"Have you talked to the guys about when we're supposed to go swimming?"

"Sam and Coop are on their way to Shawn's as we speak."

"I just need to run home and get my bathing suit," he said, thinking it would give him at least a quick chance to ice his wrist.

"Already got it," Lily said.

Great, he thought, loading the balls into the bucket, making sure he'd shut off the power on the machine.

"So we're clear on this staying between us?"

"If you ask me again," Lily said, "I may have to violate the sister version of the Bro Code."

"Honestly, Lils, it's nothing," he said.

"Really? When was the last time you were in this cage by yourself?"

"Maybe I was in the cage by myself," Ben said, "to stop my hitting from becoming a thing."

"You mean like the thing you had about Chase during basketball?" she said, raising an eyebrow at him, one of her many skills. "When you turned into a complete lunatic trying to make yourself better than him?"

"But I got over that."

"Yeah," she said, "but it took a world of hurt — for all of us — before you did."

"But I did get over it."

"Just don't make this thing with your hitting turn into something you have to get over," she said. "Deal?"

"Deal," he said.

"I mean it," Lily said.

"When was the last time you said something you didn't mean, Lils?"

"Excellent point."

After the balls were picked up and he'd locked the door to the cage, Ben bumped Lily some knuckle with his left hand, just to show her he was feeling better, forcing a smile as he did, his way of showing her that he was feeling better already.

Even though he wasn't.

He'd come here to hit and gotten hit instead — had basically found a way to hit *himself* — *and* now his wrist hurt worse than his arm had hurt after Robbie got him.

Lily didn't know how right she was.

Totally crazy.

By the next morning, after he'd bluffed his way through Saturday afternoon with his friends, Ben's left wrist was swollen to twice its normal size. He tried to grip a bat even before he had breakfast, see if he could do that without it hurting.

No shot.

He tried to keep his left wrist in his lap when he was eating his cereal, but his mom noticed it right away.

"Left hand off the table?" Beth McBain said. "You've suddenly decided to use proper table manners."

He grinned. "I knew how much it would mean to you."

"I don't think so."

"C'mon, Mom," Ben said. "How many times have you told me elbows off the table?"

"How about we make an exception?"

"I like it this way," he said. "It's the new me."

"You, sir, are hiding something," she said. "You know what they say on the cop shows: Put your hands where I can see them."

He lifted his left hand, gave her a little wave with it.

"Whoa," she said.

"Had a little accident in the cage yesterday I might have forgotten to mention."

He wasn't going to admit to her, or his dad, that he'd actually let a baseball hit him on purpose, it was bad enough having Lily know, she kept giving him looks at Shawn's pool every time she thought the guys weren't watching.

"What happened?" his dad said, putting down the sports section of the paper.

"We need to have it looked at," Ben's mom said, "even if it is a Sunday. Look how swollen it is."

"No, Mom!" Ben said. "It's not like I broke it or anything. I wasn't paying attention and took one square off the top of the wrist."

"Says young Dr. McBain," she said. "There should be a show about you on television: *Ben's Anatomy.*"

"Good one," Ben said.

"I thought so," she said.

Jeff McBain made Ben wiggle his fingers, had him make a fist, gently manipulated it one way and then another, had Ben put his palm out and push against his own.

"I basically think it's a bone bruise," Ben's dad said. "He's got too much range of motion for there to be any real damage, far as I can tell. But I am going to ask you to consider full body armor for your next game."

"Maybe an Iron Man suit," Beth McBain said.

"TV and now the movies, Mom," Ben said. "You're on a roll."

"When is your next game, by the way?" she said.

He told her tomorrow night, at Hewitt against the Giants.

"Listen," Ben said. "I know I've had a couple of bad breaks to start the season. But they're not real breaks."

"Despite the fact that I'm living with a couple of orthopedic specialists," Ben's mom said, "I'd still like to have a doctor look at my boy."

"Mom, I'm telling you, nobody knows my body better than me," Ben said.

"Even if you can't seem to get it out of the way of pitched baseballs these days," she said. "Whether they're being thrown by humans or nonhumans."

"I've just got to do a better job of getting out of the way," he said.

His dad grinned. "You *think*?"

"Next time," Ben said.

"Which won't be practice today," his dad said. "Lots of ice the rest of the day, no baseball."

"I'm still *going* to practice," Ben said. "Even if all I do is run around on the bases a little bit."

"I'm just asking," his dad said, "but do you suppose you'll be able to accomplish that without the ball finding you?"

"The parents on *Modern Family* aren't as funny as you two," Ben said, "no kidding."

"Thank you for noticing," his dad said.

His mom said, "And here I thought football was the only contact sport I had to worry about with my baby boy."

Me, too, Ben thought.

Me, too.

*   *   *

Ben didn't remember until he saw Justin at practice that he'd forgotten to call him back the day before.

Justin was warming up on the side with Darrelle, Clayton and Shawn. Ben wanted to be out there with them, but he wasn't allowed to even play catch today, parents' orders. They'd even taped his wrist, his mom saying it was as much a reminder for him not to use his left hand as anything else.

"Sorry I forgot to call you back, J," Ben said.

Then he held up his wrist, showing him the tape. "I was too busy getting a hit-by-pitch from a ball machine."

The guys stopped throwing. "You're making that up," Darrelle said.

"Wish I was."

Shawn said, "How come you didn't tell us at the pool?"

"Would you cop to something like that if you didn't have to?" Ben said.

Darrelle said, "Please tell me you're not hurt bad."

"Just my pride."

"Didn't you say before the season that one of our goals was for nobody to get hurt?" Shawn said.

"This is it for me, promise," Ben said. Then he said to Justin, "Anyway, sorry again about yesterday."

"No worries."

Justin threw the ball back to Darrelle, said he was warmed up, went over and sat down on the bench. Ben went with him.

"So what's up?" Ben said.

"Nothing."

"Must've been something," Ben said. "You wanted to come over."

Justin turned and looked right at Ben. "Now you want to talk?"

"I would've remembered to call you back," Ben said, "if I hadn't been so busy being what my dad likes to call a chowderhead."

He held up his taped wrist again and said, "No kidding, who do you think feels worse right now, you for having to miss a game or me?" Smiling as he did.

"Me," Justin Bard said in a low voice.

"C'mon," Ben said, "what did you want to talk about?"

"I told you," Justin said, "it was nothing."

"Was it about throwing the bat?" Ben said. "You just had a bad moment, is all. Happens to everybody."

"You have no idea what you're talking about," Justin said. "The worst thing that ever happens to you is getting hit by a couple of baseballs."

"That's not true," Ben said. "You saw how I scuffled going up against Chase in basketball, we were on the same team. You know it was my fault that Sam got hurt and missed most of the season. And everybody can see how messed up I am at the plate right now."

"You can come out of slumps," Justin said, staring out at the field, Sam and Coop throwing with Shawn now.

"Is there something going on you're not telling me?" Ben said. "Talk to me, man."

Still staring at the field Justin said, "I wanted to talk yesterday."

Ben said, "I'm trying to be your friend."

Justin stood up. "That's what I wanted you to be yesterday," he said, and started jogging toward the outfield, running all the way to the right-field fence and then making his way toward center.

By the time he got back, Mr. Brown said he was ready to pitch himself some serious BP.

"Who wants to hit first?" Mr. Brown said.

"I will," Justin said, batting helmet already on his head, Ben not sure if he was anxious to take some swings, or just wanted to get it over with.

Justin grabbed his bat, got into the left-hander's side of the box, took the same stance he'd been using since the first time they'd all played together, the stance he said his dad had taught him in their backyard. Feet wide apart, hands set right near his left shoulder, just the slightest waggle to his bat as he waited for Mr. Brown's first pitch.

"Okay, big man," Mr. Brown said. "Let's have some fun today."

Justin lined the first pitch he saw over first base so hard that Shawn, who was standing there, didn't even have time to get his glove up.

Then Justin hit the next pitch over the right-field fence, making everybody on the field at Highland Park whoop and holler, right before Justin hit the *next* pitch.

No smile from Justin, no change of expression. He just set the bat and waited for everybody to settle down.

"Better dial it up a little, Dad," Sam said. "He's making you look like this is slow-pitch softball."

Coop said, "That's actually kind of insulting to slow-pitch pitchers."

"Dig in, Justin," Mr. Brown said. "You're going to have to pay for the serious chirp I'm getting."

Sam, waiting to hit, said, "Chirp, Dad? Really? Please don't try to talk like us."

"I'm feelin' you on that," Mr. Brown said, and now Sam just said, "Oh God."

Justin hit the next pitch to the base of the centerfield wall, didn't even look as if he'd swung hard. Ben was totally focused on Justin now, watching how cool he was in the batter's box, how little wasted motion there was, how short his stride was. Wondering what had changed inside him since Friday night's game, when he'd looked as if he couldn't play dead. Saw how focused Justin was.

Saw no fear in him, none, as Mr. Brown did try to crank it up now.

Justin went to the opposite field this time, hit one over the left-field fence. Still not looking as if he were swinging as hard as Ben knew he could. Ben didn't know what was bothering Justin these days, why he'd acted like a stranger when Ben had tried to talk to him before, but all Ben knew watching him hit was that he would have changed places with him in a heartbeat.

Coop was behind the plate, in his catcher's gear.

"Okay, boys, Justin Bard is back," he said.

Took off his mask, grinning, being Coop, and said, "Good thing, too. We were thinking about trading you right out of town."

Justin wheeled on him, his face red, just like that, and yelled, "Shut up, Coop!

The force of it actually made Coop step back.

"Dude," he said, "I was *joking.*"

"Well, you're not funny," Justin said, his voice still way too loud, too hot for what Coop had said.

"Hey," Coop said. "Relax."

"Don't tell me to relax," Justin said.

He took a step toward Coop. Ben couldn't believe what he was watching, but he was running over from the bench as Mr. Brown came running in from behind the mound.

Justin took a step toward Coop, but Ben knew Cooper Manley well enough to know that he was through backing up.

"Hey," Coop said, "it's not *my* fault you threw *your* bat."

"I told you to shut up, Manley."

Now he was Manley.

Ben didn't have to step between them because Mr. Brown already had.

"I don't know what this is about," he said to Justin. "But I don't think Coop meant anything by what he was saying. I think you owe him an apology, Justin."

Justin, still staring at Coop, said, "You're not my father."

"No," Mr. Brown said. "But I am your coach. And I think maybe you need to take the rest of the day off."

"Fine," Justin said. One last word coming out of him hot.

He turned and walked over to the bench. Took off his helmet, dropped his bat on the ground, grabbed his glove, got on his bike, and then was gone.

Nobody on the field, not even Mr. Brown, said anything right away. They all just watched until Justin's bike had disappeared.

Finally Mr. Brown said to Sam, "You're up."

"Yeah," Sam said.

Coop said to Ben, "What was *that*?"

"Unclear," Ben McBain said. "But I'm going to find out."

Somehow find a way to be the friend today that Justin wanted him to be yesterday.

"We could go with you," Sam said to Ben after practice.

"I *should* go," Coop said. "It was my big mouth that made *his* head explode."

They were all standing near the bike rack that was between the home team's bench and the fence at Highland Park.

"It had to be more than what you said," Shawn said to Coop. "You've said a lot dumber things than that."

"A *lot*," Sam said, nodding.

"I get it, okay?" Coop said. "I get it."

"Seriously?" Shawn said. "He acted like you stole his phone."

"Or broke it," Sam said.

"I think I gotta do this myself," Ben said. "I'm the one he wanted to talk to in the first place, even if he says it was nothing."

"You don't even know if he went home," Sam said.

"Then all I did was make a trip over there," Ben said.

"It's a haul getting to his house," Coop said.

"Nothing's that much of a haul in Rockwell," Ben said.

"Call us after," Sam said, "maybe we can get pizza or something."

Ben said he would and headed off on his bike. It wasn't just him not knowing if Justin would be home or not. He didn't know if Justin would even want to talk if he was home. But he had to do something, that much he did know. Justin had freaked as much with Coop — basically over nothing — as he had throwing his bat the way he did in the Darby game.

The only times he'd ever been to Justin Bard's house was for birthday parties. It was right next to Rockwell Country Club, part of something called Country Club Estates, big houses with a gate and a little guard shack in front, the guard having to buzz you in, Ben remembered, if you didn't live there.

It was on the north side of Rockwell, from Highland Park you had to go back through town to get there, go past the high school, go all the way to the imaginary town line between Rockwell and Silver Springs. Ben didn't know how long it took him to get there from the field, didn't check the time on his phone when he left. He just knew that Coop was right. It *was* a haul. But the whole way over, he kept going over in his head the weirdness with Justin and Coop, how mad Justin had gotten. Nobody ever got that mad at Coop.

Justin had, and all because Coop had tried to give Justin a funny shout-out on the most awesome batting practice any of them had ever seen.

But why?

The only way to find out was to ask him, straight up, just

the two of them. Sam had always said there was a good reason Ben was captain of all their teams, because he was a
born leader.

Ben was being that kind of leader now.

As he finally arrived at the gate to Country Club Estates,
Ben realized that he was going to have to stop and give his
name to the guard, and that the guard would then have to ring
the house. And if Justin decided he didn't want Ben to come
all the way up to the house, then the guard shack was going
to be the same as a dead end.

But then he got a break, the gate opening for a car that
had just stopped, obviously a visitor, Ben timing it just right so
that he followed the car in, smiling and waving at the guard,
just shouting, "Friend of Justin's, he knows I'm coming."

The guard just waved. When you were eleven and Ben's
size, they clearly didn't view you as much of a security threat.

So he rode his bike up Fairway Drive, noticing again how
big the houses were in here, how much property each one of
them had, remembering that Justin's was the last one on
Fairway Drive, at the top of the hill overlooking one of the fair-
ways on the golf course, Justin telling Ben that when the
course was empty in the early evening, he and his dad — who
were members — would go out and chip golf balls, just the
two of them.

But it wasn't the size of Justin's house, at the top of that
hill, catching Ben's attention now, stopping him cold at the
bottom of the driveway.

It was the "For Sale" sign next to the mailbox.

Ben did something he never did in sports.

Hesitated.

Stay or go? He didn't know whether the sign meant that Justin was just leaving this house or leaving Rockwell. All the sign meant was that he was moving somewhere.

But if it was just a move across town, what was the big deal about that, why couldn't he have told the guys on the team? This had to be something that had just happened, the sign going up, the house going up for sale, just because everybody seemed to know everything about everybody else in Rockwell, it was that kind of small town. Even though Justin's house was a little bit out of the way, it seemed as if somebody would have known, Ben's parents always seemed to know if one of their friends had bought a new car, or sold one, or put a new coat of paint on their house.

Maybe the sign *was* new, had just gone up in the last few days, maybe that's why Justin had been acting the way he had been. Ben's mind was racing with all kinds of thoughts, questions without answers, standing there with his bike propped against his hip at the bottom of the driveway.

Thinking: What if he really is moving out of town?

Then asking himself this question: What if it were *me*? What if I was the one who'd just found out that my family was moving away from Rockwell? What if I'd just found out I was leaving the Core Four Plus One?

Leaving Sam and Coop and Shawn?

And Lily?

Ben McBain knew the answer to that one, knew he would need his friends more than ever, whether he was about to leave them or not.

He hopped back on his bike, catching his left wrist on the handlebar, feeling the quick stab of pain, but knowing in that moment that it was nothing compared to what Justin was feeling, if Ben was right about the move.

He got to the top of the driveway, laid his bike down in the grass, rang the doorbell, waited.

When the bright red front door opened, Mrs. Bard was standing there.

"Hey, Ben," she said. "This is a surprise."

"Hi, Mrs. Bard," he said. "Is Justin here?"

"Upstairs in his room," she said. "Is he expecting you?"

"Nah. I just decided to stop by, is all."

She tilted her head slightly. "Not exactly on your way home from practice. Did something else happen today?"

Ben said, "Just the usual dumb guy stuff."

True enough.

Mrs. Bard said, "I offered to drive my slugger and pick him up, but he said he wanted to take his bike. Said he needed all the exercise he can get since he doesn't get to play the next game after that little episode with the bat."

"I tried to tell him, Mrs. Bard," Ben said. "There's always a lot of dumb guy stuff going around. Lily's always telling me it's practically required if you're a guy."

From another part of the house, Ben could hear a man's

voice, probably Mr. Bard, sounding as if he were talking to somebody on the telephone.

"You want me to tell Justin you're here," his mom said, "or do you want to just go ahead up?"

"I'll head up."

"Maybe you can lighten him up," she said. "Things have been a little tense around here lately."

Ben didn't wait around to find out why, if she meant that it was because of the "For Sale" sign or because of the way Justin had been playing. And acting.

He ran up the stairs to find out, Justin's mom telling him it was the second door on the left.

"What do you want?"

That was Justin's greeting when he looked up and saw Ben. He was on his bed, long legs stretched out in front of him, pillow in his lap, laptop on the pillow.

"Can I come in?"

"Do I have a choice?" Justin said. "You're already in."

Ben thought: It's like we're strangers all of a sudden, even though we've been in school together since kindergarten.

Gone to school together and played three sports a year together since they'd started playing organized sports. And hung out together. Again: Not boys the way Ben and Sam and Coop and Shawn were boys. But Ben had always considered Justin a friend. Was trying to be his friend now.

Even though Justin wasn't making it easy.

"I felt like you might want to talk," Ben said, then put his hands up in front of his face, the way you did when you thought somebody might take a swing at you, and said, "Even though you told me before you *didn't* want to talk."

Justin sighed now, loud enough that Ben wondered if his mom could hear it downstairs, closed his laptop, tossed it on the bed beside him, Ben trying to remember the last time he had seen him smile, thinking that if he'd hit baseballs today the way Justin had, it would feel like his birthday.

"Not a good time," Justin said. "But you probably figured that out."

"You really want me to come back when it's a better time?"

"There is no better time," Justin said.

Ben took a deep breath now, let it out, said, "I saw the sign out front. Man, I'm sorry, this is an awesome house." Paused and then said, "You guys moving to another part of town?"

Hoping that was it, plenty of his friends' parents had moved from big houses into smaller ones the past few years.

"I thought you were here to talk about Coop," Justin said, ignoring the question.

"Aw, don't worry about Coop, Coop's fine," Ben said. "You know him. He hardly ever gets mad at anybody, and when he does, he doesn't stay mad for long." Ben grinned. "It requires too much concentration."

"It's just . . ." Justin stopped, shook his head. "It's just that the real estate woman just put up that sign this morning. Who knows, maybe that's why I hit the way I did at practice even though I can't hit in a game right now. Maybe I just needed to take it out on something."

Ben said, "I'm lucky right now if I can hit my pillow with my head."

"You'll be fine," Justin said. "You're always fine. You're Ben McBain."

At least we're talking, Ben thought.

"It's not always so great being me, trust me," Ben said.

"Better than being me."

Then, as if somebody had thrown a switch, he was breathing hard, really hard, his eyes red. All the things you did right before you started to cry.

The sound of his breathing was the only sound in the room now, Justin taking in air and letting it out and trying as hard as he could, Ben could see the effort in him, not to cry in front of another guy.

When Justin was able to speak again, this is what he said, the words coming out of him so weakly Ben was shocked they even made it across the room:

"My parents are getting divorced."

The boy who hadn't wanted to talk at practice talked for a long time. Like he'd been waiting to tell somebody all the things he was telling Ben.

Telling him that his dad, who traveled a lot, who had the kind of company that bought and sold other companies, had moved out during Little League season, even though Justin hadn't told anybody at school about that and nobody, even in small-town Rockwell, had found out.

"I didn't want anybody to know," Justin said. "And I kept believing my parents when they were telling me this was something they had to try. So as much as it hurt not to have my dad living in the house, I just kept telling myself that eventually they really would work things out."

He put air quotes around "work things out," hopped off his bed now, walked across the room, and shut his door.

"I kept hoping they'd do that," he said, "and that my dad would come back home to live."

Another deep breath. "But he never did."

Ben couldn't help it, he knew this wasn't about him, it was all about Justin, but he couldn't help imagining what this would be like in his room, telling somebody else that his dad had left his mom.

"At the beginning," Justin said, "they just said they needed some time apart." He closed his eyes. "Right," he said. "Try till the end of time."

"How have things been between you and your dad?" Ben said.

Thinking about his dad as he asked the question, the way things were between them, how close they were.

Feeling luckier than he ever had in his life.

"They're fine," Justin said. "He keeps telling me nothing is ever going to change between us. Except he's living on the other side of town and my mom and I are about to *leave* town."

There it was, in the air between them, the air in the room changing just like that, Ben getting the answer he'd come up here looking for, even if it wasn't the one he wanted.

He wasn't just moving.

He was leaving.

I would want to throw things, too, Ben thought, or maybe find a wall to punch.

"My mom wants us to move back to Cameron," Justin said. "It's where she grew up, you know that, right?"

Ben knew because Justin had told him when they'd gone to a sleepaway basketball camp there the summer before last. He couldn't remember exactly how long it took to get there, but it was definitely more than an hour.

"Her whole family, most of it, anyway, is still there," Justin said. "My grandma and grandpa, my aunt and her kids. And my uncle. Did you see him when you came in? My uncle, I mean. He's downstairs."

"I heard him talking on the phone," Ben said.

"He's the one who wants her to come home to live, says she needs her family."

"You're her family," Ben said. "You and your sister. But your sister's in college. You're her family and this is your home."

"I keep trying to tell everybody that!" Justin said. "But it doesn't look as if my vote counts."

In a quiet voice, Ben said, "How soon?"

"Are we leaving?"

"Yeah."

"Sometime before school," he said.

"Maybe she'll change her mind," Ben said.

Justin looked up with eyes that had stayed red the whole time. "You don't know my mom," he said. "But then, lately, I don't, either."

"This isn't between you and your mom," Ben said, trying to think of things Lily would say, wishing Lily were here to help him. Help him and, more important, help Justin.

"This is between your mom and your dad," Ben said, "and you're just caught in the middle."

"Tell me about it."

That's when he told Ben he was thinking about quitting the team.

12

They were in Ben's basement, two boxes of pizza on the table between the couch and the big screen, game-watching TV.

Ben, Lily, Sam, Coop, Shawn. Ben had texted everybody as soon as he was back at the bottom of the driveway, told them to meet him at his house, called his mom and dad to make sure it was all right and ask them to have the pizza delivered, telling them he'd explain everything when he got home.

He had done that. His mom said she had no idea, his dad said the same thing, both of them wanting to know how Justin was doing.

"Bad," Ben had said.

Now in the basement, after Ben had given his best friends in the world the play-by-play, Lily said, "Well, you can't let him quit. Seems to me like he needs you guys more than ever."

"I told him pretty much the same thing," Ben said. "He said his mind was made up."

"Not only does he need you guys," Lily said, "I think he needs baseball, too."

"Could have fooled me," Coop said. "I mean, now I know why he's been acting like a jerk. But he's still been acting like a jerk. So if he does need our help, he's had a funny way of showing it."

"You're forgetting that I was a bigger jerk than he ever thought of being in football," Shawn said. "Creeps me out just thinking about it."

"That was because you were getting crushed by the pressure from your dad," Coop said.

"Right, genius," Ben said. "Now multiply that by two. Justin's getting crushed by *both* his parents, just in a different way than Shawn was."

Sam was staring at Coop. "Are you really this thick?"

Coop held up a finger. "Okay, maybe I *was* thick. But now that you guys are explaining it to me, I feel less thick."

"Yeah," Lily said, "thin, practically."

"Bottom line?" Sam said. "Lily's right, we gotta do *something*."

"You think about it," Lily said. "If he didn't have baseball right now, even the way he's been playing, what would he have?"

"Pretty much the worst summer of his entire life," Ben said.

"Maybe we can't save his summer," Sam Brown said. "But we at least have to try."

Lily smiled then, one of her biggest and brightest Lily smiles, stood up, walked in front of each one of them, bumped each one of them some hard knuckle.

"You only do that when you think you're about to be brilliant," Ben said.

"Well, that's just plain old wrong," she said. "Because then I'd be doing it all the time."

"What you got, Lils?" Sam said.

"I think," she said, "that maybe we're about to become the Core Four Plus *Two*."

When Lily and the guys had gone home on Sunday night, Ben went upstairs and talked about it with his mom, his dad still off playing in his Sunday night softball league.

She was in the den watching her favorite television show, *Downton Abbey*, about a bunch of English people living in some kind of castle.

Beth McBain paused the show as soon as she saw Ben standing in the doorway.

"Mom," he said, "this can wait, I forgot it was *Downtown* time."

"You know it's pronounced *Down*-ton," she said. "But you've got that face."

"What face?"

"The face you get when you're trying to save the world," she said, "usually one kid at a time."

"Justin," he said.

She patted the couch next to her. "Step into my office and have a seat," she said.

He told her about Lily's plan, saying that was the best they could come up with, for them to basically take Justin in, and then somehow convince him that cutting himself off from the team wasn't going to help him hurt any less.

And would probably hurt him more.

"I know I've asked this question before," Ben's mom said, "but are we absolutely certain that girl is only eleven years old?"

"You just say that because she reminds you of what you were like when you were eleven."

"Well, there is *that*." She took off the glasses she wore for television and driving a car — and watching Ben's games — and said, "Sounds like you've got this under control. So what do you need your old mom for?"

Ben said, "I'm just trying to figure out why Justin's mom would do this to him?"

"Get divorced? Sweetheart, I hate to be the one to tell you this, but half the marriages in our country end up in divorce."

"No way."

"Way sad," she said. "But way true."

"I'm not really talking about the divorce part, though, Mom. I don't even know whose fault that is."

"Maybe it's no one's fault," she said. "Maybe it just took this long for Justin's mom and dad to figure out that they're not supposed to be married to each other. Like I said, big boy: It just happens sometimes."

"But why does she have to leave town?" Ben said. "Why does *that* have to happen?"

"I don't have the answer to that one," she said. "But I'm sure it must be a very difficult decision for her, at a very difficult time of her life. And even though Marcy isn't a close friend, I know how much she loves her son, so she must think this is the best thing for both of them."

Ben looked at the TV screen, frozen on the face of some old woman he thought might be the Queen of England.

"Justin sure doesn't think it's the best thing for both of them."

"Don't imagine he would."

"I've *got* to help him, Mom."

"No doubt in my mind that you will," Beth McBain said. "And bringing him into the world's coolest club for eleven-year-olds on the whole planet seems like a pretty cool way to start."

Ben reached over then and hugged his mom, even though she was the one who usually initiated the hugging, pressed his face into her shoulder. It was a good thing, because she didn't see how he clenched up his face when his sore wrist got pressed between her back and the back of the couch.

"Don't you and Dad ever get divorced, okay?" he said.

"Not happening," she said, kissing the top of his head.

"Promise?"

"Promise," she said in a quiet voice. "In fact, I can guarantee you that you and your father will always be together."

"How?"

"Because he informed me a long time ago that even if I ever left him, he was going with me, that's why!" And smiled.

Then she pointed her remote at the screen and told him lights-out by ten o'clock.

"Thanks," he said.

"Wow," she said. "Usually you don't thank me for reminding you about your bedtime."

"Thanks for listening."

"Didn't really do much more than that."

"Then how come I feel better than I did when I came in here?"

"Because sometimes," she said, "just the thought of helping somebody makes you feel good before you actually help them. Now let me get back to my show, they've got problems of their own to solve."

From the doorway Ben said, "If any of them come up with a better idea for Justin, gimme a shout."

"Hush," his mom said, "I think the two old grandmas are about to have a throw-down."

"You make it sound like wrestling," Ben said.

"It kind of is," she said. "Just with English accents. Everything always sounds better with English accents."

Ben told her that maybe he'd try that with Justin.

13

Ben called Justin when he got up, Justin actually answered his phone for a change, asked him if he wanted to hang out.

"I'm with my dad today," he said.

Ben said, "You thought anymore about what we talked about yesterday?"

"About quitting?" Justin said. "I don't have to think about it anymore."

"Because your mind's still made up."

"Pretty much."

"Will you make me one promise?" Ben said. "Will you promise me you won't do anything before we talk about it again?"

"You mean like tell Mr. Brown?"

"Like that?"

There was a long pause at Justin's end of the phone until he finally said, "Deal."

Ben said, "Even though we're on the phone, we're shaking on this, okay?"

"You're a little weird sometimes, you know that, right?"

"Only with my friends," Ben said. "Are we shaking on this or not?"

"We are," Justin said.

Ben's wrist was still sore, he still couldn't grip a bat the way he wanted to. Or needed to. But no way he was missing the game, not after he'd injured himself in the cage. He didn't even let his dad tape the wrist, telling his dad that he was fine, smiling away — and through the pain — as he twisted it this way and that to show his dad he was ready to go.

He knew he could catch the ball at short, knew he could close the game if Mr. Brown asked him to do that. And figured that he could find a way to work a walk or two, get on base, use his legs the way he always had to help his team win.

They were down a man already because of Justin's suspension — maybe down a man permanently if Ben couldn't convince him to stay on the team — and so Ben was going to play, even if he had to convince everybody, and himself, that he was feeling a whole lot better than he was.

Sometimes his mom would get off the phone after talking in this sweet voice to someone Ben knew she didn't like all that much, a smile on her face the whole time, and say to him, "What can I tell you, hon? Sometimes you have to fake a little sincerity."

That was Ben tonight in Hewitt, the game 5–5 when Ben led off the top of the sixth, his hitting no better than his wrist. He'd led off the game by opening up his left side way too soon, left knee buckling again, hitting a soft liner to the second baseman, knowing the swing had nothing to do with his wrist being sore.

Just afraid.

Still.

At least he'd worked a walk last time up, stole second, making sure to go in feet first, hands high, taking no chances going in headfirst, which Mr. Brown hated, anyway. Then he'd stolen third the same way and scored on a sac fly from Sam.

Now he was up in the top of the last, unless they went extra innings, tie game, waving at strike one. The new Hewitt pitcher wasn't exactly throwing sidearm, more like three-quarters. But it was more than enough to make Ben miss.

The kid threw him two balls after that, both outside, trying to get Ben to chase. Ben fouled off the next pitch, then swung and missed — badly — at strike two, the Hewitt kid going outside again, maybe seeing that Ben had no chance at a pitch off the outside part of the plate the way he was swinging the bat.

Ben swung and missed again.

Ball three was up in his eyes.

Full count.

And Ben made up his mind what he was going to do if the next pitch was anywhere close to the plate. Tired of waiting to be a real hitter again, the hitter he used to be. Tired of going up there and hoping — or begging — for a walk.

It was going to be a borderline pitch, maybe on the outside corner, maybe not, Ben didn't care. He dropped the handle of his bat, made sure not to cross the plate too soon, and pushed a perfect two-strike bunt to the left of the pitcher's mound.

Ben knew that fouling it off was strike three, same as missing it would have been strike three. But he still trusted himself to get a bunt down even if he couldn't get a clean hit these days and came out of the box flying, seeing that he'd pushed the ball just hard enough to get it past the pitcher — kid dove for it, missed — and just soft enough to keep it on the infield grass.

Ben saw all that, saw the second baseman get a late break on the ball, never thinking that Ben would bunt with two strikes. Then Ben was only concentrating on the first-base bag, prepared to launch himself headfirst this time even if that did mean banging the bad wrist in the dirt.

But he didn't have to.

Because the Hewitt second baseman, who should have eaten the ball, who should have seen that Ben had the play beaten, tried to make an off-balance throw even when Ben was across the bag and threw wildly, over Ben's head and over the first baseman's head and into foul territory down the right-field line.

Way down the right-field line.

"Go!" his dad was yelling from behind him, from the first-base coaching box, but Ben didn't need anybody to tell him that, he was already turning for second.

Already thinking about third, the way he did when he was running from first on a single to right.

Picking up Mr. Brown in the third-base coaching box as he got near second base, Mr. Brown windmilling his left arm. Telling him to come on.

Ben cut the second-base bag perfectly, dropping his left shoulder, leaning into the cut like he was in the open field in football, not sure where the ball was behind him, not sure if it was in the air yet or not.

Just knowing that it wasn't going to beat him to third.

Maybe he couldn't hit a ball right now, but he knew he could sure outrun it.

He picked up Mr. Brown again as he got to third, saw that he was halfway down the line between third and home, telling Ben he didn't have to slide. Ben made the turn, kept coming toward Mr. Brown, allowing himself a look across the diamond, realizing now the ball must have rolled a long way in right because the second baseman — who must have gone out to take the cutoff throw — still had the ball in his bare hand.

Standing in short right, not so far beyond the infield dirt. Long way from home plate for a second baseman's arm. The kid trying to decide whether to run it the rest of the way in, or just throw home, Ben still only a third of the way down the line, if that.

Almost like the second baseman was waiting for Ben to make the first move, like in this moment it was a game of baseball chicken.

And that hesitation was all Ben needed, not waiting for Mr. Brown to tell him what to do, knowing what he was going to do, knowing that he was going home, running right past Sam Brown's dad, Darrelle in the on-deck circle telling Ben to slide, Ben doing just that, crossing home plate on the seat of his pants with the run that put the Rams ahead in the top of the last inning in Hewitt.

It hadn't been a real home run, the kind that a guy like Justin Bard could hit, the kind that cleared the fence with ease and just kept rolling.

But somehow the crazy trip Ben had just made around the bases made it feel like one.

He high-fived Sam and Coop and Shawn and the rest of the guys waiting for him in front of the bench, kept the celebration to just that, telling them to stop jumping around, the game wasn't over yet.

"Home Run McBain," Coop said when they all finally sat down, Ben still breathing hard.

"Shortest in history," Ben said.

"Hey," Sam said, "stop calling yourself short."

"You know what I mean," Coop said. "If you can't hit, you go to plan B. For *bunt.*"

"If we were the home team," Shawn said, "would they call it a walk-off run or a *run*-off run?"

"We're not the home team," Ben said. "So let's hope we get a few more runs this inning and then three more outs."

"Which you're going to get for us," Ben's dad said, having

jogged in while Sam got ready to hit, Darrelle having struck out. "The coach wants you to start warming up." Jeff McBain grinned. "Unless you're too tired."

"Dad?" Ben said. "I'm going to forget I heard that last part," and went looking for his glove. Warmed up with Coop, went out and pitched a one-two-three bottom of the sixth, two ground balls and a pop-out to Shawn, playing first tonight instead of Justin Bard, game over.

Now Ben allowed himself to celebrate with his teammates for real in front of their bench, Mr. Brown coming over and sticking the game ball in the pocket of Ben's glove.

"All sorts of ways to win a ball game," he said.

"Figured I better get on base any way I could," Ben said, "especially the way I've been going. And if there's one thing I know I can still do, it's get a bunt down. Figured it put me more in charge than the pitcher."

"Still," Mr. Brown said, shaking his head. "A two-strike bunt? In what could have been our last ups? Seriously?"

"You're always telling us that baseball isn't supposed to be serious, it's supposed to be fun."

"Got me there," his coach said. "I'm always telling Sam that every game I watch I still hope I'm going to see something I've never seen before. And guess what? I just did."

Then Mr. Brown told the rest of the guys to head out into short left-field for their postgame sit-down, one they always had, home or away.

Ben walked between Sam and Coop, both of them still talking about the walk-off bunt. Or run-off bunt. Whatever it had been, other than a little hit that turned into just big fun.

"Wish I had a stopwatch on you," Coop said, "just to see how long it took from the time you bunted the ball until you slid across the plate."

"He did slow down a little rounding third," Sam said, "so maybe it wasn't world-record time."

Ben took one last look across the field then, trying to picture himself making his way around the bases, seeing the Hewitt kids in front of their own bench having their snack.

Then he stopped, because beyond the Hewitt bench and the fence behind it, he was sure he saw Justin Bard turn and start walking across the parking lot, in the direction of the truck where people could get drinks and ice cream and candy, the same kind that parked outside the field in Highland Park for Rams' home games.

No way, Ben thought.

Why would Justin have come all the way to Hewitt and not let anybody know he was there to watch the team play?

Better question: Why would he come all the way to Hewitt to watch a team he said he was going to quit?

"Hey," Ben said to Sam and Coop, who were a few yards ahead of him.

They stopped.

"What up?" Sam said. "What you lookin' at?"

"I could have sworn I just saw Justin," Ben said.

"Where?" Coop said. "Or maybe you've just got Justin on the brain right now."

Ben pointed in the direction of the snack truck. By then the kid, whoever he was, Justin or somebody else, had disappeared.

Ben waited until he got back from Hewitt to text Justin, wanting to find out if he'd been at the game, but trying to make it funny.

U see my pathetic version of one of your homers?

No response.

Maybe he wasn't back yet. And even though Ben's friends usually had their phones with them at all times — Coop slept with his under his pillow, afraid he might miss a message — maybe Justin left his at home sometimes. Or had lost it. Or had just turned it off.

Or maybe he was looking right at the screen on his phone when Ben texted him and just didn't want to talk to him. Ben knew: Sometimes no response was just about the loudest response to a text you could get.

Basically telling you to leave them alone.

But Ben knew that was a great big no-can-do. Justin needed him even if he didn't know that. Or wouldn't admit that. He needed a friend, needed his teammates, needed baseball.

What Ben needed?

More of a plan than just asking Justin to come hang out with Ben and Lily and the guys. A plan that would work as well as plan B — for bunt — had worked against the Hewitt Giants.

He tried calling Justin after breakfast the next morning, got no answer, texted him again.

Want to hang out later?

Took his phone with him upstairs, fired up his laptop, checking out the box scores from last night's baseball games, wanting to see how the guys on his fantasy team had done, Ben and Sam and Coop and Shawn having a team together in a sixth-grade fantasy league. But Ben had loved box scores even before he was in a fantasy league, loved the way they could tell you the story of a game you hadn't even seen. Loved how neat they were, even if the game had been messy.

Box scores making a lot more sense than real life did sometimes.

But he kept looking down at his phone, knowing that if it had been Lily or Sam or Coop or Shawn, the response to one of his texts could come so quickly it was almost as if they hadn't typed out any words, as if the thought had come directly from their brains.

Still nothing from Justin except loud silence.

He knew he couldn't go over to his house, just show up again, not because it was such a crazy long bike ride, just because he'd tried that approach already and even though he'd found out what was bothering Justin, he hadn't been able to get through to him. Like it was football and he thought he saw an opening and then got dropped as soon as he tried to run through it.

So come up with another play, he thought.

But *what* play?

Man, he thought, summer wasn't supposed to be this hard, summer was supposed to be easy. *Aggressively* easy, was the way Coop put it.

How do you help somebody who acted as if the last thing he wanted in the world was your help?

And then it came to him. Ben smiled, feeling as brilliant as Lily Wyatt, and sent Justin Bard another text.

This time he got a response.

Justin was waiting for him at the batting cage when Ben got there, little before noon, Justin having told him in his text back he couldn't make it before then.

"Just so we're straight," he said, "this doesn't change anything."

"Good morning to you, too," Ben said. Smiling.

"You know what I mean. I didn't come here to listen to you try to talk me out of bagging the season."

"Not why I asked you here."

"So we *are* straight?"

"Totally."

Justin wouldn't let it go.

"'Cause if you tricked me into coming, then we're like the opposite of straight."

"I got you over here for the exact reason I told you," Ben said. "I need your help."

"I read your text."

"I can't hit anymore," Ben said.

"I know," Justin said. "That *was* me at the game last night."

Ben knew Justin well enough to know that he said exactly what he meant. And meant what he said. So Ben *wasn't* going to push him about the team, at least not today. The Rams didn't have another game for a couple of days, their second game against Robbie Burnett and Parkerville, on Friday night in Parkerville. Plenty of time.

For now, he was just happy that Justin was here with him. Trying to be a friend to Ben. That was all the plan Ben had, turn the thing around, let Justin try to help him, not make Justin feel like some kind of charity case.

Let him try to pick Ben up.

And if he did, if he somehow could help Ben with his hitting, all the better, just because Ben was the one feeling like a charity case these days when he was trying to get a real base hit.

The first thing Justin told him was that they didn't need the cage, at least not right now. He picked up his bat bag, looking a lot fuller than it usually did, and told Ben they were going to use the empty field closest to them at Highland Park.

"What's in the bag?" Ben said.

"Stuff."

"Stuff?"

"Don't worry about what's in the bag," Justin said. "We've got a lot of work to do."

Ben grinned. "Mr. Brown is a lot more fun as a coach than you are, and we haven't even started yet."

"We're not here to have fun," Justin said. No change of expression. "We're here to teach you how to hit again."

"I looked that bad last night?"

"You've looked that bad since Robbie hit you," Justin said. "A two-strike bunt? Are you joking?"

"I was desperate," Ben said.

"That's not the word I would have used," Justin said. "Now come on. I did some studying on this before I came."

"For real?"

"Your problems can be fixed," he said, and then led Ben across the outfield.

When they got to the infield, Justin dropped his bag near the pitcher's mound, got out a half-dozen scuffed baseballs, told Ben to go get in the batter's box. Ben did as he was told, dropped his own bat bag near the on-deck circle, started to pull out his bat.

"Leave the bat," Justin said.

"Batting practice without a bat?" Ben said. "Why didn't I think of that?"

"You can use your bat later," Justin said.

"This is what you learned from your research?" Ben said.

"I also called my dad," Justin said. "He knows more about hitting than anybody I know. He told me that we should really do what we're gonna do for a couple of days. But I told him you pick up things quicker than that."

"Thanks," Ben said. "I think."

"Don't thank me yet," Justin said. "Now get in there and take your stance and I want you just to do one thing when I start pitching. Two things, actually. Watch the ball. And no matter what, don't move."

"And this is going to help me . . . how?"

"You're going to go back to focusing on the only thing that matters to a hitter," Justin said. "The ball."

"What if the ball's going to hit me?"

"Then you can move," Justin said. "But it won't hit you. When's the last time you remember me making a throwing error?"

"Never."

"Because I never have," Justin said. "Now let's go to work."

For the next half hour, that's all they did, Justin pitched and Ben watched. The only time they stopped was every six pitches, Ben picking up the balls in front of the screen and tossing them back to him. Neither one of them spoke. Ben wondered what people passing by walking dogs, moms taking small children to the playground, must have thought, watching baseball like this, a batter without a bat.

Finally Ben said, "Am I allowed to ask how long we're going to do this?"

"When you stop flinching completely."

"I haven't been."

"Really?"

"Maybe a couple of times when the ball was inside."

Justin held up the ball, like he was showing it to him, and said, "When this makes you stop flinching."

About ten minutes later, Ben picking up the balls again, Justin said they were good. Walked down toward the plate.

"How come you don't duck every time you throw a pitch in a game?" he said to Ben. "Ever wonder about that? A ball can come back at you harder than you're throwing it. Lot harder sometimes."

Ben said, "The only thing that makes sense to me is that when I'm pitching, I feel like I'm the one in control."

Justin pointed at him. "Which is *exactly* the way I feel when I've got a bat in my hands. And the way you used to feel, I bet."

"You're right," Ben said. "Now what's next?"

"Wiffle balls!" Justin said.

"Now those I know I can hit."

Justin shook his head, actually smiling for the first time all day, like he was starting to enjoy himself even though Ben wasn't. Looking in that moment like the Justin Ben used to know.

"No hitting yet. More watching."

Ben groaned. Justin shrugged. "Hey," he said, "you're the one who asked for help."

"Yeah," Ben said. "Be careful what you ask for."

"Did all these drills come from your dad?"

"Some of them," he said. "Then he told me about this website to check out."

"And did the website say how many pitches I'm supposed to study before I get to swing at any of them?"

"They say a few hundred," Justin said.

"*What?*"

"Don't worry, McBain. I like you. But I don't like you *that* much."

He took his stance with a bat and watched Justin throw Wiffle balls. Then the old tennis balls he pulled out of his bat bag. Every few minutes, Justin would throw one of the tennis balls right at Ben. With purpose. Ben got out of the way every time.

When they stopped for a water break, Ben checking his cell phone and seeing they'd been at it for more than an hour and a half, he asked Justin if his arm was getting tired.

"What difference does it make?" he said. "You're the pitcher, not me." Paused and said, "I'm not anything anymore."

"Can I say something about that?"

"No."

"Just about baseball," Ben said, and before Justin could stop him he said, "If you didn't love baseball the way you do, you wouldn't have called your dad and you wouldn't have found these drills and you wouldn't be doing them with me."

Justin took a long drink of water, nearly finishing half of the big plastic bottle he'd brought with him.

"You think too much, McBain," he said. "It's part of the problem you're having with hitting right now, you're thinking too much and that's the worst thing a hitter can do." He looked out across the field now, like his eyes were fixed on a point beyond the outfield walls. "Another thing my dad always taught me."

Ben didn't say anything. Justin took another swig of water and said, "*Now* we go to the cage."

The two of them grabbed their bat bags, walked past the pitcher's mound, past second base, back across the outfield, opened the little door in the wall in left-center, next to the sign that said "Rockwell YMCA." Headed back to the batting cage. Ben not sure in that moment which one of them needed the other more.

But then thinking this:

If you really were friends, what did it matter?

It was three o'clock when they finished in the cage, Ben having finished what had become the longest baseball practice of his life, hitting one line drive after another.

Actually thinking he *was* seeing the ball better because of Justin's drills.

"You look a lot better," Justin said, helping him pick up balls.

"I was hitting well in the cage before," Ben said.

"But not like today."

"Not like today."

"The last two buckets, you didn't jump one time," Justin said. "Not anything like your at bats last night."

"It was really that bad?"

Justin nodded.

"I notice stuff like that," he said, "even if Mr. Brown and your dad didn't. My dad . . ." This time when he said it, he managed a small smile. "I don't know if you know how great a hitter he was, right until he tore up his knee his junior year at UConn, came back, and then tore it up again."

"Must run in the family," Ben said. "The hitting part, not the knee part."

"I guess," Justin said, looking off again. "Anyway, the first coaching he ever gave me in the backyard on hitting was the best: See ball, hit ball."

"Whoa," Ben said, "that is *way* too complicated for me."

And Justin laughed.

They picked up the balls, Ben locked the cage, they walked toward where their bikes were leaning against the fence.

"You think I got this now?"

Justin said, "Truth?"

Ben nodded.

"I think it's gonna take more than one day to un-mess you up. It's gotta happen in a real game, against a real pitcher."

"Like the one we're facing Friday night?"

Justin said, "If not against him, then who?"

"Thanks, Coach."

"I'm not your coach."

"Could've fooled me today."

"I just couldn't stand there and do nothing when you *were* that messed up."

Same, Ben thought.

He said to Justin, "You want to come over to my house and get something to eat and just hang the rest of the afternoon?"

"On one condition."

"Name it. I owe you for today."

"No, you don't."

"What condition?"

"No more baseball today," he said. "And no more talk about baseball."

Ben said he was down with that, he actually had a different sport in mind for the rest of the afternoon.

17

Pickup basketball at the new and improved McBain Field.

Improved by Ben's dad, who had surprised him when the snow was finally gone and it was really spring again in Rockwell. His dad said he was having a new basketball court installed at the small park all the kids in town really did think of as belonging to Ben, even though it still officially belonged to the town of Rockwell.

"Can't have star players stepping in any more holes out there," Jeff McBain had said at the time.

Obviously talking about what had happened to Sam during the basketball season.

"That was my fault, not the court's," Ben had said. "If I hadn't kept him out there that night, he couldn't've stepped in that stupid hole."

"Right. And that pothole I drove into on Route 5 the other day, that must have been *my* fault," his dad had said. "Anyway, I'm happy to spring for this, I look at it as an investment in your future, and mine."

"Yours?"

"Yup. You've got a lot more years ahead of you on that court, and being able to look out the window and watch you will give me almost as much happiness as it'll give you."

It was called a VersaCourt and it was a cool blue color, white lines for the free throw lane and foul line and even the three-point line they were going to use in high school someday.

"It's . . . perfect," Coop had said when it was finished, the first time they were allowed to play on it. And they had played a bunch of pickup games during the spring, even when they were playing their Little League season. But they had all been so fixed on summer baseball no one had even suggested playing hoops since school let out.

Until today.

It made perfect sense to Ben, just because the last time Justin had really been Justin was during basketball, way before his dad had moved out or his mom and dad had talked to him about divorce. Way before Justin had found out he was leaving his school, his friends, his teams. Leaving the only life he'd ever known.

Playing a game of basketball wasn't going to change that, or make it any easier for Ben to really put himself in Justin's shoes.

For one afternoon, he just wanted them all to be in basketball shoes.

Ben and Justin had gotten to the court at McBain after Ben's mom had fixed them a snack. They walked across the grass where the Core Four guys still played Home Run Derby with Wiffle balls, passed the swings where Ben and Lily still did some of their best talking, came up on the basketball court — *half*court, really — that still looked brand spanking new, starting shooting around while they waited for Sam and Coop and Shawn and Lily to show up.

"Don't tell Lily that I asked," Justin said, "but is she a good enough basketball player that the sides will be even?"

Ben said, "I *won't* tell her you asked, because that would be a bad thing for you. Extremely bad. The kind of bad that would make being grounded for life seem good."

"I get that," Justin said. "But you didn't answer my question."

"You're telling me you've never seen any of her girls' games?"

"Heck no," Justin said.

It was amazing how many of his boys had zero interest in girls' sports, whether Lily Wyatt was playing them or not.

"Lily," Ben said, "can seriously play."

"*You're* serious?"

"Totally," Ben said. "She's Lily. Can you imagine her not being great at something?"

"Good point."

When everyone had arrived at McBain, they decided to make the teams Ben, Sam, and Lily against Shawn, Coop, and Justin.

"You sure these teams are fair?" Shawn said. "We've got a lot more size."

"You have size," Lily said, "but we have superior speed, intelligence, shooting ability. And looks."

She was wearing a LeBron T-shirt, but from when he was still with the Cavaliers, had her hair in a ponytail, looked happier than anybody on the court at McBain Field.

"We also have Ben and Sam," she said.

"If LeBron's the 'King,'" Coop said to Justin, "Lily thinks she's the 'Queen.'"

"Only until they change the rules and girls can be king," she said.

They decided to play games of eleven baskets, had to win by two, winners out. Sam guarded Shawn, Ben took Justin, Lily asked if she could guard Coop, even though he really did have a huge size advantage on her.

"You know I'm gonna post you up," Justin said to Ben. "Just letting you know in advance."

Grinning at him. Maybe Lily wasn't the happiest one here, maybe Justin was, just because he was away from baseball, everything that baseball seemed to represent to him right now.

"And I," Ben said, "am going to make you chase me until you beg for a water break. Just like when we play smalls against bigs in practice during the season."

"What is it about you guys?" Lily said. "Are we gonna trash-talk or are we gonna play?"

"We call it chirp," Coop said.

She made a sniffing sound and said, "But it *smells* like trash."

Ben's team won the first game 11–8, making their last three shots, Lily making the winner, from beyond the three-point line. Ben drove toward the basket, everybody on the other team thinking he was either going to shoot himself, or feed Sam. But Lily was wide open outside the three-point line, Coop tired from chasing *her*. Ben wheeled at the last second, threw the ball out to her, all she had to do was make the shot. Which she did, before breaking into her own dance version of the Harlem Shake.

Justin said to Ben, "Does she always get like this?"

Ben said, "Only when we can settle her down."

Justin's team came back to win the second game, though, mostly because both Justin and Coop got hot. Ben had been a little worried about how things would be with the two of them, because of the blowup on the field that day, but both of them acted as if it never happened, high-fiving each other after one of them would make another shot.

They were the Core Four Plus Two on this day, just the way Lily wanted them to be, nobody talking about baseball, or Justin's move, just laughing and hooping and having summer feel the way it was supposed to when you were eleven.

They took a water break and decided the next game would be their last. Ben and Lily sat under the basket, the other guys sat in the shade of the big tree beyond the hoop.

"Justin seems to be having a good time," Lily said in a voice only Ben could hear.

"Great time."

"I really am a genius," she said.

Ben said, "You think you're a genius when we let you pick the toppings on the pizza."

She turned and looked at him, face serious. "Sausage and

mushrooms are better than pepperoni," she said. "It's just a fact, McBain."

Ben had been thinking that it wouldn't be the worst thing in the world if Justin's team won the third game, even if they had to let him do it. But it turned out he didn't need any help. He got even hotter now, like somehow this was the basketball version of batting practice, and he couldn't miss here, either.

Laughing sometimes when he'd make another crazy shot, not trying to show up Ben's team, just because he was stupidly on fire.

But he finally missed when it was 10–6 and then it was Sam who got hot, hitting three in a row. Then Ben faked to Sam, drove right past Justin, made it 10–10.

Now Sam missed a wide-open jumper, Coop rebounded, started to feed Justin, saw that Ben was covering him all the way outside the three-point line, fed Shawn instead. Shawn leaned into Sam, then faded away, made a sweet jumper of his own.

Point game.

Justin ended up with the ball on the outside, him against Ben. No thought of letting Justin or his team win. It had seemed like a nice idea. Ben knew he wasn't wired that way, even when he was basically playing in his own backyard.

By now he knew Justin's game: He liked starting on the left side, where he was now, because then he could drive right. And once he started driving, he usually went all the way to the basket. But if he started dribbling left — he had a good left hand for a guy who didn't have to do much ballhandling on their town team — he was looking to pull up and make one more jumper, the way he'd been making jumpers all afternoon.

He started driving right, big first step, getting his shoulder past Ben. But Sam left Shawn and came over, cutting him off, and Lily picked up Shawn. Coop was open, but too far away from the basket at that moment to be a threat.

Justin in the lane now, Ben on his hip, Sam in front of him. Justin should have passed, probably *would* have passed in a real game. But this wasn't a real game, and he *had* been stupidly hot. And so he was going to take the last shot.

He went up and Sam, who could jump better than anybody in town their age, went up with him, arms straight up in the air, daring Justin to shoot over him.

Justin didn't even try.

For the first time all day he switched the ball to his left hand, and shot it *around* Sam Brown, one of the mutt-ugliest shots Ben had ever seen in his life.

One that somehow hit softly off the square painted behind the basket and dropped through the net to make it 12–10.

Lily looked at Justin, hands on hips, and said, "You have *got* to be joking."

"I would have even been embarrassed to *call* bank on that shot," Sam said.

Shawn and Coop? They were just pointing at Lily now, and laughing, and doing their own clumsy version of the Harlem Shake.

Then Ben and Sam and Lily couldn't help themselves, they were laughing, too, making complete fools of themselves because of Justin Bard's fool shot to beat them.

The only one not laughing, not doing anything, just standing there, was the guy who had made the shot.

He had gone to retrieve the ball and was just standing there in the grass, staring at the rest of them, ball on his hip. Ben thinking in that moment how lonely he looked, even though he was right there.

When Justin saw Ben staring at *him*, he said, "I can't."

"You mean laugh?" Ben said. "Man, you've *got* to laugh at a shot like that."

Justin put the ball down. Not just looking lonely. Looking to Ben, to all of them, like the saddest kid in town.

Everybody stopped laughing now, everybody seeing what Ben had seen on Justin's face, nobody making a sound at McBain Field, all the noise and fun of the afternoon, of the last shot, suddenly gone.

Finally Lily said, "Justin, what's the matter?"

"Everything," he said, then turned and ran toward Ben's house, where he'd left his bike near the front walk, running as fast as Ben had ever seen him.

Ben started to run after him. Justin was fast. But not that fast.

Lily put a hand on his arm.

"I don't get it," Ben said.

"I think I do," Lily said. "All of us being this happy just made him more sad about leaving."

They could see Justin already on his bike now, heading up the street, until he was out of sight.

Ben thinking that Justin kept finding different ways to leave this summer, maybe practicing for when he finally had to leave for good.

Justin didn't reply to text messages the next couple of days. So after all the progress Ben thought they'd made, they were back to that. The only good news was that Sam's dad hadn't said anything about Justin telling him that he was quitting the team.

So nobody knew if Justin was going to show up in Parkerville on Friday night or not, even late Friday afternoon,

Ben and the guys in his basement, just killing time until Ben's dad would drive them all to Parkerville for their seven o'clock game.

"No way he shows," Coop said.

He was playing MVP Baseball against Shawn, but it didn't stop him from talking. Sam liked to say that Coop's voice would be able to survive a nuclear attack.

Now Sam said, "That's the first encouraging thing I've heard."

"What?" Coop said, fingers working his controller, face serious.

"You saying he won't show," Sam said. "Now I think he will."

"Me, too," Ben said. "But I only ever bet on the way I want things to work out."

"I'm with Sam and Ben," Shawn said.

"Three against one," Coop said. "Shocker."

"Look on the bright side," Ben said. "It still adds up to four. As in Core Four!"

"Whatever," Coop said, tossing his controller aside, Justin Verlander striking out Bryce Harper in the bottom of the ninth, Coop's team beating Shawn's. "I can take all of you."

"What we need to do tonight," Sam said, "is take down Robbie Burnett. We're stressing so much on Justin, we're kind of forgetting that."

"I'm not," Ben said.

"Sam's right," Coop said. "Payback time tonight."

"I wish," Ben said.

"You *know*," Sam said. "You started one season off wrong because of Robbie. Tonight you get a do-over."

"You're sure about that?" Ben said.

"We're all sure," Sam said.

Ben looked at all of them, sitting on his couch. They all nodded back at him.

"Sure thing," Coop said.

"Justin may not show up in Parkerville," Sam said. "But you will."

They both did.

Justin's dad brought him.

They showed up just a few minutes after Ben and the guys had piled out of Mr. McBain's new SUV, Mr. Bard walking with Justin over to the bleachers on the third-base side of the field, chatting briefly with Ben's dad and Sam's, calling over to Justin and telling him he'd be back, he was going for an iced coffee at Dunkin' Donuts.

Justin said, "Don't get lost, Dad."

"Never," his dad said.

Ben was on the bench, switching from his sneakers to his baseball shoes when Justin came and sat down next to him.

"Talk to you for a second?" Justin said, and nodded in the direction of left field.

"Sure," Ben said, not even waiting to lace up his shoes, just walking with Justin toward the outfield.

When they were far enough away from the rest of the Rams, Justin said, "My dad talked me out of quitting."

Ben smiled at him. "Good!"

"He reminded me that being on a team doesn't just involve playing, it involves responsibility. And accountability. He's always been big on both those things."

"Same with my dad," Ben said. "For pretty much my whole life."

"He said that you don't just let your teammates down when you quit, you let yourself down."

Ben nodded.

"Just wanted you to understand why I'm here," Justin said.

"I do."

"My dad said you only stopped playing if you were too hurt to play. And he said that didn't involve hurt feelings."

Ben waited, sensing that he hadn't said everything he'd come out here to say.

He hadn't.

"I didn't want to say this in front of Sam and the other guys," Justin said. "But since my dad knew what you'd been going through, he said that if I just up and walked away, I'd be letting you down, too."

"I want you to play because you want to play," Ben said, "not because of me."

"My dad said that nothing that's happening to me is baseball's fault, basically."

"It's not with me, either, if you really think about it."

"You ready to face Robbie tonight?"

"Better be."

"You're going to figure it out, wait and see."

Ben put out his fist, Justin bumped it, Ben said, "How about we try to figure everything out together?"

Justin said that sounded good to him, he wasn't doing a very good job of figuring things out for himself lately.

Robbie Burnett came over before the game, wanted to know how Ben's arm was.

Ben flexed and said, "Perfect."

"I still can't believe I hit you in the first game of the season," Robbie said.

"As long as you don't do it tonight," Ben said, smiling, "then we're good."

Then Robbie told him he wasn't starting tonight, they were going with their other best pitcher, a lefty named Frankie Henson, and that Robbie was scheduled to pitch the last two innings.

"That's when I'm really dangerous," Robbie said, smiling back, "as a closer."

"The arm you need to worry about is my *right* arm tonight," Ben said, "because I'm closing, too."

"Then it's on."

"So on," Ben said.

He had a good batting practice, Justin making sure he hit behind Ben, watching every swing Ben took against Mr. Brown.

Every few pitches Ben would hear him say, "Watch."

Ben finished with a line drive up the middle that went whistling past Mr. Brown's head, laid down his bunt, deadening the ball perfectly, ran it out hard, because he always did, went to get his glove.

Reminding himself of what Sam said about the season starting over tonight. A do-over against Parkerville, against Robbie. But telling himself not to worry about having to stand in there against Robbie Burnett later, just telling himself to worry about the first pitch he was going to see, top of the first, against Frankie Henson.

"See ball, hit ball," Justin said as Ben was putting on his batting helmet.

"Sounds simple enough."

"Because it *is* simple enough," Justin said.

Ben walked to the plate, tapped the shin guards of the Parkerville catcher tonight, another kid he knew from football named Tim Barrett, got ready to hit. Not looking to take a strike, the way he sometimes did his first time up, looking to take a rip at the first good pitch he saw, knowing he wasn't going good enough to lay off what might be the best pitch he was going to see the entire at bat.

Maybe it was because Frankie was the first lefty he had seen all season, maybe because the ball was coming at him from the first-base side. Or maybe — just maybe — it was all the work he'd done with Justin.

Whatever it was, Ben hit Frankie Henson's first pitch of the game on a line over the second baseman's head for what felt like the first really clean hit he'd had since he'd *been* hit.

He thought about stomping the first-base bag the way guys did home plate after a big home run, it felt that good to finally put a bat on the ball that way. But he didn't, he did what he'd been taught to do, cut the base, made the turn, even faked like he might try for second as their right fielder came up throwing. Came back to the bag. Took a low five from his dad, who leaned close to him and told him he was stealing on the first pitch to Darrelle.

It was then that Ben took a quick look across the field to the Rams' bench, saw Justin shaking a fist at him, then smiling and pointing to his own eyes.

See ball, hit ball.

Ben stole second, Darrelle singled him home two pitches later, Sam doubled down the left-field line scoring Darrelle with the Rams' second run. Frankie against Justin now. Lefty against lefty. Justin's first official at bat since he'd gotten bounced for throwing his bat.

Parkerville might have needed a big-league lefty like David Price to get Justin out in that moment. Or CC Sabathia. Justin hit a 1-1 pitch from Frankie Henson over the right-field fence at what was called Parkerville Memorial Park. It was 4–0, Rockwell, and Frankie Henson still hadn't gotten anybody out.

When Justin got to the bench Ben said, "The only time I can't see the ball is when you hit one out of sight."

It was 5–0, Rams, by the time the top of the first ended, Shawn doubling after Justin's homer and Coop singling him home before Frankie Henson struck out the three guys at the bottom of the Rams' order.

But then Kevin Nolti, starting for the Rams tonight, got banged around the way they'd just banged around Frankie. Worse, actually, Parkerville not only scoring six runs in the bottom of the inning but leaving the bases loaded. Ben felt like the game had been going on for an hour, and they were only getting ready for the top of the second.

Coop said, "What was the score the last time we played these guys in football? It's gonna end up like that."

"Are you kidding?" Shawn said. "It's going to be closer to the final score in basketball."

By the time Robbie Burnett came in to pitch the first one-two-three inning, top of the fifth, the score was 10–10. Ben had gotten one more hit, off the right-handed pitcher who came in to replace Frankie, walked the other two times he'd been up, scored four runs by now.

But now he needed somebody to get on for the Rams in the top of the sixth, because he was scheduled to bat fourth in the inning. Not only were the Rams going to need at least one base runner to have a chance to go ahead in this game — that was if Ben could hold Parkerville in the bottom of the fifth — they needed at least one base runner so that Ben could face Robbie.

Suddenly the only thing making him afraid on this night was that he *wouldn't* get to face the guy who'd made him afraid in the first place.

Afraid in baseball for the first time in his life.

It meant he was feeling like a ballplayer again, the kind he'd always been.

First things first, he did have to hold Parkerville in the bottom of the fifth.

Then Ben promptly gave up a hit to Robbie, who then stole second, barely beating Coop's throw. But Ben pinned him there, striking out the next two guys. Frankie Henson now. Ben got the count to 1-2, thought he could make Frankie chase a pitch that was nearly in the dirt for strike three. Instead Frankie stuck out his bat, and managed to hit a soft liner to center field.

Robbie was running with two outs, Ben was slapping his glove hard against his thigh, knowing the game was about to be 11–10 for Parkerville.

Would have been 11–10 if somebody other than Sam Brown was playing center field.

Ben turned and saw that Sam had closed so fast on the ball, with his amazing speed, that he was picking it up just a few feet beyond the infield dirt, fielding it in perfect stride, the transfer out of his glove happening as fast as everything else was at Parkerville Memorial Park, coming up throwing to the plate.

The rules in their league were you couldn't come into home plate standing up if there was going to be a play there. Coop got himself into perfect position blocking the plate as Robbie came hard down the line, Coop as fearless as he was funny.

Sam's throw came to him on the fly, a perfect throw to Coop's glove side, Coop not even having to turn his body to catch it.

The play that should have made it 11–10 for Robbie and Parkerville wasn't even close, Coop waiting for Robbie's slide, his bare hand on the ball in the pocket of his catcher's mitt, knowing that the only bad thing that could happen was Robbie sliding into the glove and knocking the ball loose.

The home plate umpire had come around to Coop's left, to have the best possible look at the plate, immediately threw up his right hand, and yelled "Out!"

Unbelievable throw, unbelievable play.

When Ben turned to see where Sam was, he saw that Sam Brown was already at their bench, he'd tell Ben later he never stopped running after he made his throw, knowing that Robbie had no chance, never doubting that the inning was over and the game was still tied.

That was just Sam.

When Ben got over to him, the two of them touched gloves and Sam grinned and said, "Just so you know, Robbie still hasn't touched home plate."

Then Cooper Manley was with them, his face mask tipped back on his head, his helmet in his hand, smiling the way he always smiled when sports felt like this, like it was the Core Four against the world.

"Only boneheads," Coop said, "think they can run on Sam's arm and *through* me."

Sam looked at Ben now, his manner all business, because there was still work to be done.

"We softened Robbie up," he said. "Now you finish him off."

Justin was there, too, looking at his arm like he was looking at an imaginary wristwatch. "I believe it's payback time," he said.

Then it didn't look as if Ben would get the chance, not unless the game went into extra innings. Robbie got two fast outs in the top of the last, looking as if he were throwing even harder than he had in the opening game. Getting the ball from their catcher, barely waiting, in such a good rhythm he looked almost impatient to throw his next pitch.

Before Ben left the bench for the on-deck circle, two outs now for the Rams, Justin came over to him. "Step out on him. It will throw him off a little, trust me."

Ben nodded. "Got it."

Justin said, "All's we need is a base runner."

Ben said, "If Steve gets on, I'm getting a hit off this guy, I know it."

Steve Novak was a new kid, having just moved to town after spring break for Rockwell Middle School. He was a decent enough player, but Mr. Brown had him batting tenth tonight, because you were allowed to bat ten in their league. Steve was really fast, could play any position on the field except catcher. But he always seemed to hit better in batting practice than he did in games.

Bottom line? Wasn't an accident he was hitting at the bottom of the order.

Somehow, though, he fouled a couple of pitches off at 2-2, worked the count full on Robbie Burnett. And when Robbie didn't get a call he wanted with his 3-2 pitch, a ball at the knees, Steve Novak had gotten a walk off him.

Ben exhaled for the first time since Robbie had delivered his 3-2 pitch, walked to the plate. Took a great big deep breath now.

And got ready to face Robbie Burnett again.

Sam and Coop and Shawn — and Justin — knew how much this at bat meant to him. So there was no loud chatter from any of them. The only voice he heard now was Justin Bard's, telling him, "Be a hitter."

Yeah, Ben told himself.

Be a hitter.

If he was ever going to be one again, it had to start right here, against this pitcher. The one who'd put him down hard.

Time to get back up.

See it, hit it, see it, hit it.

Hard.

The first pitch from Robbie was so far outside that Tim Barrett, the Parkerville catcher, didn't even touch it with his mitt, the ball going all the way to the screen, Steve Novak having to do nothing more than jog down to second base, you were only allowed one base on a wild pitch to the screen.

Go-ahead run on second.

Ben looked out at Robbie, mad at himself for wild-pitching Steve into scoring position, Ben thinking that somehow Robbie looked more nervous in this moment than he was. Maybe throwing a pitch that far outside because he was afraid to come in on Ben after what had happened in the opener.

But Robbie came right in with a fastball down the middle, and Ben took it for strike one. As much as he wanted to swing the bat on this guy, the ballplayer in him made him force Robbie to throw a strike after missing that badly.

1-and-1.

Now Ben asked the ump for time, stepped out the way Justin had told him to, leaned down and tied a shoelace that absolutely did not need tying. Took another deep breath. Got back into the box, took his stance.

This time Robbie came inside on him, the kind of inside pitch that had been turning Ben's front knee to jelly since he'd gotten hit.

Just not this time.

He saw it all the way, knew that as far inside as it was, it wasn't far enough inside to hit him. Ben saw the ball that well coming out of Robbie's hand. He just *knew*, after watching what felt like a couple of hundred pitches from Justin at Highland Park that day.

So Ben just calmly raised his arms, leaned back in that cool way Jeter did with inside pitches, just sucking in his gut and sticking his butt out. Just not moving his feet.

Not bailing out this time.

Not even against Robbie Burnett.

2-and-1.

Ben thought about stepping out on him again, didn't, just stepped right into the next pitch he saw, a Robbie fastball about belt high. Stepped right at Robbie with his front foot, not toward third base or the Rams' bench or downtown Parkerville, stepped into that fastball and drilled it into left-center, a screamer up the gap, one Ben knew was going to roll all the way to the wall.

Steve Novak scored easily, Ben stopped at second even though he was sure he could have made third, Mr. Brown having a big thing about never making the last out of the inning or the first out of the inning at third base.

So he stopped at second, even though in that moment Ben felt like he was home.

Home free.

Ben hoped that Darrelle would find a way to keep the inning going, get Sam to the plate and maybe Justin, bust the game wide open so that he wouldn't have to pitch the bottom of the sixth with a one-run lead, not that he ever minded doing that.

But Darrelle struck out swinging, a 3-2 Robbie fastball up in his eyes, like Darrelle had decided to swing no matter where the pitch was.

Ben jogged toward the Rams' bench, not to celebrate his hit, no interest in that, still too much work to do. Just like that he had to go from being a hitter — on the night when he felt like a hitter again — to being a pitcher.

When he had his glove, he made sure to run alongside Justin so he could say, "Thank you."

"For what?" Justin said. "Being the kind of teammate you are?"

"You still didn't have to do it, you have enough going on."

Justin said, "Yeah, I did."

He went to first, started throwing grounders to the infield-ers while Ben warmed up with Coop. No chatter from Coop now, he always knew when to be all business.

All Coop did when Ben had finished with his warm-up pitches was to make a quick patting motion with his mitt. Take it easy. Coop knew Ben well enough to know how pumped he'd been when he got to second base, knew how much Ben had been going through even if the two of them hadn't talked about it, Coop and Sam and Shawn knowing this was something Ben had wanted to work out for himself.

Not knowing about Justin showing up to coach Ben that day, like he was a friend coming out of the bull pen.

Now Ben was the bull pen guy, in a real game, a close game, a chance to make the run he'd knocked in stand up by getting three more outs.

Coop, being Coop, did have one comment he wanted to make, jogging out to the mound and saying, "A one-two-three inning would be gorgeous," then heading back to the plate before Ben even had a chance to respond.

It turned out to be a one-two-three inning, Ben having already pitched through Robbie and their best hitters in the bottom of the fifth.

He struck out their catcher, Tim Barrett, on three pitches.

Got their third baseman to hit a slow roller to Justin at first, Justin having to take just a few steps before he stomped on the bag, hard.

Two away.

Justin could have tossed the ball to Ben, decided instead to come over to the mound. "Finish this," he said, stuffing the ball into the pocket of Ben's glove like he was spiking it.

Parkerville's right fielder, Tommy Monahan, at the plate. Saw three Ben McBain fastballs, all of which had a little something extra on them. Tommy swung at the first, took the second for strike two, swung through a strike three it looked like he missed by a foot.

This time it was Coop, who'd sprinted out to the mound, who spiked the ball into Ben's glove and said, "Totally gorgeous."

But when Sam got to the pitcher's mound from center field, Ben immediately handed the ball to him, saying, "This is yours. You don't make that throw, we don't win this game."

Justin pushed Ben's cap from behind, down over his eyes, and said, "Game over, slump over."

They walked off the field together, Ben and Justin leading the way, Sam and Coop and Shawn behind them. Mr. Brown was waiting for them in front of the bench, along with Ben's dad. They both high-fived him. Then the Rockwell Rams were ripping into the homemade cookies and drinks that Steve Novak's mom had brought, Mr. Brown telling them to eat up and drink up, he wanted to have their sit-down in the outfield and then get everybody on their way back to Rockwell.

"Good night to be a Rockwell Ram," he said.

Great night, Ben thought, feeling pretty great himself.

They sat in the grass on a summer night and ate cookies and replayed the game, even knowing Mr. Brown would be doing the same thing in a few minutes: Sam's throw. Ben's hit. Coop's catch and tag at the plate.

"You know what I think that tag was?" Ben said to Sam. "I think it was gorgeous."

"Hey," Coop said, "that's my word."

Ben looked past his teammates now, saw Mr. Bard leaning against the fence, Justin with him, Justin looking even happier to be with his dad on this night than he had been beating Parkerville.

More than any of them, he looked like he didn't want the night to end.

The way, Ben thought to himself, he wasn't going to want this summer to end.

The one promise Justin had gotten out of his mom was that they wouldn't move before the end of the Rams' season, even if the Rams made it all the way to the state tournament for eleven-year-olds.

Other than that he didn't have an exact date. One day before Justin showed up for practice Coop said it was like one of those disaster movies where you knew the world was supposed to come to an end, you just didn't know when.

But Justin kept showing up for practices, was still batting cleanup for them, hitting as well as he ever had as the Rams started to string wins together and play themselves into a tie for first place — three-way tie, with Parkerville and Moreland — at the top of the Butler County League.

Somehow, though, away from baseball Justin always seemed to have something to do when Ben would ask him to come over and hang out. Or go swimming at Shawn's. Or just meet in town for ice cream or pizza or a movie.

Or just more hanging out.

"It's like he's still here but already gone," Ben said to Lily one afternoon after they'd been swimming at Shawn's.

"I hear you," she said. "He ended up not quitting the team, but it's like he's quitting everything else a little bit at a time."

They were on the swings at McBain Field, just the two of them.

"If it was me," Ben said, "I'd want to be with you and Sam and Coop and Shawn as much as I possibly could."

"You wouldn't have any choice, I'd make you."

"Oh, like I always do what you tell me to do," Ben said.

"Oh," Lily said, "like you *don't*."

Ben said, "You know, I'm not nearly as afraid of you as you think I am."

"Keep telling yourself that, McBain. You just keep telling yourself that."

"What I really keep telling myself," he said, "is that there's more we should be doing to help Justin."

"Not if he doesn't want us to, you can't," Lily said.

"When has that ever stopped us if we thought something was really important?"

"You saw what happened when we all played basketball," she said. "Sometimes helping hurts."

"Justin helped me with baseball," Ben said, "and that just helped."

Lily smiled at him. "I know you want the world to work the way sports does, where if you try hard you win. But sometimes it just doesn't."

"It would make things a lot easier."

They stopped talking now and rocked slowly in the swings, neither one of them wanting to talk just to talk. Ben could sit like this with Sam, the two of them watching a game in the McBains' basement, and not feel as if they had to be having a nonstop conversation. Not with Coop. Never with Coop. If he had a thought inside his head, it just had to come out. Even if he wasn't with you and he had a thought he wanted to share, he'd text it immediately.

Cooper Manley did not believe in holding anything back. Sometimes Ben thought Coop was afraid of quiet the way some kids were afraid of the dark.

It was Lily who finally spoke again.

"One thing Justin has to know is that you're still going to be his friend," she said. "That we'll all be his friends no matter where he lives or goes to school."

"He must know that already."

"Tell him, anyway."

"Telling me what to do again?"

"Absolutely!" Lily said.

"I'll tell him when I see him at practice, it's not something you tell a guy in a text."

"Okay," she said, "just don't put it off."

"Yes, ma'am."

"Don't you *ma'am* me, McBain," she said. "When's your next practice?"

"Thursday."

"Do it then."

But Ben didn't have to wait that long. When he came in for dinner after Lily had gone home, Beth McBain told him she'd invited Justin and his mom over for dinner the next night.

When they showed up Justin whispered to Ben, "Was this you?"

Ben shook his head. "A mom deal all the way, I swear."

Ben's dad did the cooking on the grill, steak and some kind of fish and even vegetables, even though Ben just thought grilling vegetables was a way of disguising them.

Once they sat down to dinner, Ben waited to see how long it would take for the subject of Mrs. Bard and Justin moving to Cameron would take. But mostly it was the two moms talking about summer, and how summer was supposed to be some kind of break from all the running around they did during the school year and then when summer did come around, they felt like they were moving faster than ever.

"Like somebody changed the speed on the treadmill without telling us," Ben's mom said.

Justin's mom smiled. "That's exactly how I feel these days: Going faster than ever, but going nowhere."

Just to Cameron, Ben thought.

"I wouldn't ever presume to give you advice," Beth McBain said, "but when you get off the treadmill, just try to take things one step at a time."

"My mom just says it a different way," Marcy Bard said. "One foot in front of the other."

There was a pause, as if nobody knew where to go with this next. Then Justin's mom said, "Thanks for having my boy and me over tonight. Some of my friends act as if I've come down with something, even though all we're doing is moving on to the next chapter of our lives."

Justin was staring down at his plate as she said that, probably thinking it was the next chapter of a book he didn't want to be reading.

Now his mom reached over and covered his hand with hers as she said, "I've put an awful lot on this guy. But I keep telling him we'll get through it together. Right?"

"Right," Justin said.

Still staring down at his plate.

"Justin knows that when we finally settle in Cameron, he'll be surrounded by family," Marcy Bard said. "It's a good thing, he's always been so close to his cousins."

Was she trying to convince Justin of that, or herself?

"Plus," she said, "I'm going to have to get back to work at some point, and there's a wonderful opportunity that's opened up back home."

Justin gave a quick look at Ben, mouthing the word *home*.

His mom's home, not his.

Then she was telling him about how she'd worked at a women's clothing store in Cameron before she'd met Justin's dad, had studied design in college in New York City before that, a place called Parsons School of Design.

"Not only is the store still there," she said, "but it turns out my old boss is looking for a partner."

"Well, that sounds wonderful," Ben's mom said.

Ben looked at Justin, pushing vegetables around on his plate, before he looked at Mrs. Bard and said, "Why don't you just open a store here?" Ben was smiling as he said it, wanting to make sure the grown-ups at the table knew he wasn't trying to be rude or disrespectful. "That way I don't lose a teammate." He looked at Justin again and said, "Or a friend."

"Ben McBain!" his mom said.

But Ben saw his dad grinning at him from the other end of the dinner table. Maybe because one of Jeff McBain's favorite expressions was about putting things *on* the table. And that is exactly what Ben had just done.

So he kept going.

"Our friend Coop was saying the other day," Ben said, talking fast, "how he just wants to stay eleven forever, how he likes things just the way they are. And I'm not saying that Justin and I want to do that, right, J?"

Justin said, "Kind of looking forward to twelve right now, to tell you the truth."

Ben said, "But even though I know you guys are going through some bad stuff, I just hate to see Justin have to give up so much good because of it."

His mom turned to Justin's mom and said, "We encourage Ben to be honest. But clearly he's still learning to pick his spots."

Mrs. Bard didn't seem upset about what Ben had said, just looked at him and said, "Believe me when I tell you, Ben, I wish we could keep things exactly the same in Justin's life. But we can't."

"And I think Ben understands that," Ben's mom said. "Don't you, *Ben*?"

Stepping on his name so hard Ben half expected it to break.

"Mom," he said, "you're the one who always taught me that there's nothing more important than being a good friend. Or having one. I just don't want to *lose* a friend without a fight, that's all I'm saying."

In a voice so low that Ben wasn't sure anybody at the table but him heard it, Justin said, "Same."

"And we all love that about you," Beth McBain said, "when it's your fight. And this isn't, dear."

"But thank you for being so honest," Mrs. Bard said.

"You're welcome," Ben said.

Then, because he couldn't help himself — or maybe because he didn't want to help himself — Ben said, "I'm just trying to figure out if you're leaving because you have to or because you want to?"

And she said, "Maybe it's a little bit of both."

It was then that Ben's mom put her hands together like she was putting a period at the end of a sentence — or maybe closing this chapter of tonight's dinner — and said, "Who's for homemade apple pie and ice cream?"

After the dessert plates had been cleared, Ben's parents and Justin's mom went into the living room for coffee. Probably relieved, Ben thought, to be ditching *me*.

Ben and Justin went up to Ben's room.

"Wow," Justin said as soon as the door was closed.

"Wow what?"

"I can't believe the way you took it right to my mom."

"Was that a bad thing?"

"Are you *joking*? It was awesome."

"I meant every word I said."

"You always do," Justin said. "Thanks for trying."

"I didn't plan to. Once that stuff started coming out of my big mouth, it was like I couldn't stop it. You think it helped at all?"

"No," Justin said. "Nothing you can say, nothing I can say, nothing anybody can say."

"But why *can't* she have her own store here if she wants to have a store?"

"She says there are too many memories here, whatever that means."

"What about your memories?" Ben said.

Then he was talking fast again, because it wasn't the kind of stuff that guys liked to say to guys, telling Justin they were going to stay friends, no matter what, that Justin should not even try to get out of *that*.

When he finished Justin said, "Thanks for that, too."

From downstairs they heard Justin's mom calling him, telling him it was time to go home.

"Yeah," Justin said, "home for a few more weeks."

Ben didn't say anything to that because he wasn't sure there was anything *to* say to that, not in a home nobody was asking him to leave, a home that had both his parents living in it.

Ben said, "I'm the one who should be thanking you, from now till the end of the season, after the way you got me straightened out hitting."

"You would've figured it out on your own," Justin said.

"Don't be so sure."

"Come on," Justin said, "you always figure out stuff in the end."

"Not everything," Ben said.

Wanting to add: Not for you.

22

Ben and Justin made a deal: From now on they'd try to focus on something they could do something about, which meant winning one more championship together if they could.

"Control what you can control" was the way Ben's dad put it.

They couldn't do anything about Justin moving. What they could do was win their league and qualify for the states.

Some places, Ben knew, had eleven- and twelve-year-olds in the same league. But the two ages were split up in the Butler County League. Next year, when they were all twelve, they'd get their shot to play their way out of their league and all the way to Williamsport, Pennsylvania, and the Little League World Series, which only one Rockwell team had ever done in the history of the town.

It figured that this year the state tournament for eleven-year-olds was going to be played in Cameron.

"Great," Justin said to Ben. "If we do win the states, I won't even have to come back here. I'll just stay in Cameron."

"Let's worry about that later," Ben said, "and just do what Mr. Brown is always telling us to do. Enjoy the ride."

"You're right," Justin said. "Every time I say I want to stop talking about moving I find a way to start talking about it all over again."

They were stretching in the outfield grass at Highland Park before their game against Moreland. Deep into the season now, a 10–2 record, Ben couldn't even remember their last loss, six games left in the regular season, still tied for first place. There were a couple more teams in the league for baseball than in the other sports, ten in all, Moreland being one of them. The top four made the playoffs, single elimination.

"Hey," Coop said now to Justin, "I've got an idea."

"Pay attention," Sam said, "they don't come along very often with him."

"What are you talking about?" Coop said. "I'm full of ideas."

Ben said, "I believe Sam meant good ones."

"Ignore them," Coop said to Justin. "My idea is that I'll do the talking for both of us the rest of the season, and you just hit."

"It won't be hard," Sam said, grinning. "You already do the talking for all of us."

Meaning the Core Four.

"Just look at it this way, because the tournament *is* in Cameron, this time when you go there, we'll all be going with you."

They were going with their best pitching tonight. Three innings from Sam, two from Shawn, Ben for the sixth. The Moreland Tigers now had the same record as the Rams did, and had their own ace starting for them tonight, a kid named

Kyle Rafalski. Because the Rams didn't play Moreland in either football or basketball, and because this was their first game against Moreland as deep as they were into the season, this was going to be their first look at him.

"The intel on him," Coop said as they were walking to the bench, "is that he's given up one earned run all season."

"Tell me you didn't say that," Sam said.

"I know," Coop said. "A guy who can give up just one run in this league must be nasty."

"I *meant*," Sam said, "tell me you didn't say 'intel.'"

Even Justin laughed. Ben thought he seemed better tonight than usual, maybe just because it was a big game for them, against a good team, first place on the line even if there was still a lot of season left. The stands on the Rockwell side of the field, first-base side, were full, the weather was great.

All baseball tonight.

Ben said to Justin, "You ready?"

"I want to play well tonight," he said.

"You always do," Ben said.

"But especially tonight," Justin said, and then pointed to the stands and said, "Check out the top row."

Ben stopped and looked up there and saw both of Justin's parents, sitting together for the first time all season.

"Cool," Ben said.

"I don't know why it makes me feel good," Justin said. "But it does."

Ben said, "Don't worry, we got this."

Ben himself had been on a rip since the Parkerville game, now thinking of himself as having an off night when he only got one hit, usually getting at least two. After all the overthinking and worrying he'd done after getting drilled by Robbie, the game felt easy to him again, he was back to being what he'd always prided himself on being in baseball, from the time they took the ball off the tee:

A tough out.

And maybe, because of what it had taken him to get here, he was a tougher out than ever.

Sam breezed through the top of the first with two strikeouts before he faced Kyle Rafalski, who worked him to a full count before hitting a very long foul ball over the fence in left. Couple of feet from being a home run. Maybe it would have bothered somebody else. Not Sam. He was so good at sports, all sports, it was like he was always looking for new challenges, because they were new ways for him to make sports fun.

Sometimes Ben would watch him and think that Sam was playing a whole different game within the one everybody else was playing, just to keep himself entertained. So after what had been a pretty epic foul ball, Sam just got a new ball from the ump, turned, and looked at Ben at short as he rubbed up the ball. Smiling at him.

Like this was big fun now.

Turned around and blew a fastball past Kyle Rafalski for strike three to end the top of the first.

When they got back to the bench Ben said to Sam, "We

spent all that time before the game about wanting to see what Kyle's got. Only he can't possibly have what *you've* got."

"Hated to have to work that hard in the top of the first," he said. "But that foul ball annoyed me."

"Remind me never to annoy you," Ben said.

"Go get a hit and annoy *him*."

Kyle Rafalski threw as hard as anybody they'd seen this season, but didn't have the best control, maybe that's why nobody could hit off him, he made you stay loose. He kept throwing one screamer after another to Ben, Ben taking every one, working the count full himself, thinking he already should have walked after he felt Kyle had missed with a 2-2 pitch the home plate ump decided to call a strike.

But when he did get a fastball down the middle on 3-2, Ben hit a hard grounder between short and third for a clean single into left.

Darrelle popped out to first on the first pitch *he* saw from Kyle, but then Sam doubled down the left-field line, Mr. Brown holding Ben at third. Justin followed that by hitting a ball so hard right up the middle that it was past Kyle Rafalski before he could even get his glove up.

It was 2–0, Rams.

For some reason Ben found himself looking up at Justin's parents, both of them standing and clapping, his dad pointing to Justin out at second base. Then Ben's eyes found his own mom, standing with Lily, cheering for him.

Ben thinking in that moment that he was even luckier than he knew.

Was he ever.

It turned out to be a great game.

The Tigers finally tied it with two runs off Shawn in the fourth. The Rams went ahead in the bottom of the inning, Coop hitting his first home run of the season. When he got back to the bench he said to Justin, "Oh, so *that's* what it feels like being you."

Tigers came back with another run off Shawn, a two-out error from Darrelle at third, what should have been the third out, a one-hopper to him right near the third-base bag that he just dropped making the transfer from his glove. But then the Rams tied them again in the bottom of the fifth, Ben singling home Cal with a two-out single to center.

So it was 4–4 going into the sixth, Mr. Brown already having told Ben that he was pitching two innings if they went to extra innings, the rule in the Butler County League being that they only played one extra inning before the game was called a tie.

"It won't go to the seventh, Coach," Ben said. "We're winning this in our last ups."

"Which I guess means that you're going to keep the game at 4–4."

"Well, *yeah*," Ben said.

He knew Kyle Rafalski was scheduled to hit fourth in the inning, which meant that the only way he got any more swings tonight — he had singled off Sam and then doubled off Shawn — was if the Tigers got a base runner. Which they did when Darrelle, who'd moved over to short when Ben came in to pitch, made another error, throwing error this time, with one out.

The kid stole second while Ben was in the process of striking out the Tigers' catcher.

Two outs, Ben against Kyle, go-ahead run on second. Coop called time, came jogging out to the mound.

"If we get behind, a walk wouldn't be the worst thing in the world here," Coop said. "The next guy up? I know he's batting cleanup, but the guy's a total fraud. He couldn't catch up with Sam's fastball, so he's not gonna catch up with yours."

"Nice chatting with you," Ben said, grinning at him.

"I'm not saying you're *gonna* get behind," Coop said. "But if you *do*, I say we pitch around this guy."

Now Ben didn't say anything, both of them hearing the ump say, "Let's wrap this up, gentlemen."

Coop looked at Ben, grinning himself now. "We're going right after him, aren't we?"

Ben nodded.

Coop said, "Wasted a trip out here, didn't I?"

"Kind of," Ben said.

Coop took his place behind the plate. Kyle dug in. He looked like a right-handed version of Justin. Hands set just as high. Wide stance. Still as a statue once he was ready.

Ben threw a fastball right past him, Kyle taking a huge swing, trying to hit a home run, swinging so hard his helmet spun around on his head.

Ben waited for him to straighten it. Feeling his heart inside him but feeling calm at the same time. Knowing he had this guy. Going right after him. It was the funny thing about the season he'd had: Even as bad as he'd looked with a bat in his own hands until Justin had gotten him turned around, he was pitching better than he ever had in his life.

And harder.

Threw too hard now, way too hard, Coop having to come out of his crouch, nearly jumping to keep the ball from flying past him and going all the way to the screen and sending the kid at second to third base.

Coop came out in front of the plate, tossed the ball back to Ben, and smiled at him and said, "We're sort of not going for distance here."

"Got it," Ben said.

Smiled back at him. Knowing this kind of moment, against a guy this good, game on the line — this was why you played.

This was sports right here between him and Kyle Rafalski of the Moreland Tigers. His best against Kyle's best, just the air between them.

Ben took a deep breath, turned, and looked at the runner, thinking the guy wasn't going to run, try to steal third, not with his team's best hitter at the plate, Coop already having thrown out two guys trying to steal third in this game.

Ben poured strike two past Kyle Rafalski. More of a controlled swing this time than on strike one. Same result. Now he had gotten behind on him, now he was ahead in the count, now Ben threw him one more fastball, belt high, lit him up

157

one last time, Kyle missing this one — by a lot — the way he'd missed the first two.

Ben ran off the field, drinking in great big gulps of that air.

Yeah, he thought.

Yeah.

This was why you played.

23

The Tigers brought in their left fielder, Ben had heard his teammates call him Brian, to pitch the bottom of the sixth, game still tied at 4–all.

Brian was the biggest player on their team. It didn't mean he had a big arm. You could never tell by just looking at somebody. It was like trying to know the size of their heart.

Ben knew better than anybody. About arms and about heart.

Justin was leading off for the Rams, Sam having ended the bottom of the fifth with a monster fly ball to left that Brian had caught with his back brushing up against the left-field wall, Ben sure when Sam hit it that it was gone.

But it was all right.

Because Ben was sure Justin was about to do something great.

He wasn't one of those guys who thought sports was always supposed to be fair, his dad was always explaining to him that there had never been any law passed saying that sports had to be fair, or that it ever owed you anything, or that it was supposed to come out a certain way so that the good guys always won.

But Ben wanted Justin to hit one about ten miles now and win the game as much as he *wanted* this game.

He wanted Justin to have this night.

Brian threw him two balls, Justin took strike one, went after the 2-1 pitch and just missed it, fouling it back into the parking lot.

It had been a night of good fastballs in this game, Sam's and Kyle's and Ben's in the top of the sixth. But Brian had one, too, Ben could hear it just by the sound it had made in his catcher's glove. And maybe after Justin had missed at 1-1, maybe Brian thought Justin couldn't catch up with his best pitch.

And maybe he didn't know how much stick Justin Bard really had.

But now he threw Justin a fastball between his belt and "Rams" on the front of his white home jersey. And this time when Ben heard the sound of the bat on the ball — and even after being wrong about Sam's shot — he really was sure that he was hearing the sound of a home run being hit.

The Tigers' center fielder heard what everybody else heard, saw the ball come off the bat, turned and started running, what would have been a terrific jump if the ball was going to stay in the park.

Only it wasn't.

It was why the kid, tracking the ball with his eyes, stopped before he got to the warning track and then did what everybody else did, whether they were standing in front of the bench the way Ben and the Rams were, or in the top row of the bleachers:

Watched as the ball cleared the wall, cleared it by a lot, watched as long a home run as Ben had ever seen at Highland Park.

Justin didn't sprint around the bases, because that was one way of showing up a pitcher. Didn't take it real slow, because that was even a worse form of showboating. What Ben's dad called Cadillac-ing back in the day.

He just ran at his normal home-run pace, as if hitting a rocket to the moon like that was the most normal thing in the world.

Ben watching him and thinking that for this one moment sports had worked out the way it was supposed to for Justin, for this one night things were the way he wanted them to be, and not just in baseball.

They were three games from the end of the regular season, a 12–3 record now the Rams' winning streak having ended with a loss to Darby when Chase Braggs — loving every minute — retired the last nine Rams' batters of the game, finally striking out Ben to end it.

After the game Chase, chirping as much as ever, said to Ben, "You guys do *not* want to see me in the playoffs."

"Don't you mean *hear* you?" Sam said.

"My dad says that if you don't blow your horn, there isn't any music," Chase said.

When he was gone Ben grinned and said to Sam, "Well, that explains a *lot*!"

But as loud as Chase was, and as cocky as he was — he was the kind of kid Coop called a "foot long," meaning foot-long hot dog — they knew he wasn't the loudest and cockiest player in their league, because that title belonged to Kingsland's best pitcher, Pat Seeley.

"Wow," Shawn said when they were warming up on Kingsland's field, playing them on a Sunday night, starting the last week of the regular season. "Seeley's got to be the only guy in the league with shoes and a glove to match his hair."

"The shoes are a much brighter red," Sam said. "Totally."

Ben said, "You think they glow in the dark?"

And Coop said, "He probably thinks the field is named after him and not his father."

It really was called Seeley Field, and was probably the nicest field they played on all season, even nicer than Highland Park, even though Ben and Sam and the guys hated to admit that.

They knew by now that Pat Seeley's dad wasn't just his coach, he was the richest man in Kingsland, Ben's dad saying one time that Mr. Seeley didn't have to change the name of the town, because he just assumed people would know he was the king of it. Maybe that was why Pat Seeley acted the way he did, like he was some kind of prince.

The only time they had to play against him was in baseball every year. Pat Seeley played soccer in the fall and hockey in the winter, Kingsland being much more of a hockey town than basketball. But they saw him two times every summer and knew they would see him again if Kingsland made the play-offs, even though the Knights were in fifth place heading into the last week.

Coop always referred to their regular season games against Pat Seeley as the "two most obnoxious nights of summer."

It was a weird schedule, because this was the first time they'd seen Pat or the Knights, and would play them against next Friday night at Highland Park, last game before the playoffs.

Across the field, they could see Pat Seeley talking to a couple of his teammates, laughing and pointing over to where the Rams were stretching, wagging a finger when he saw them watching him.

"Not in my house!" he yelled across the field at them.

"Did he really just say that?" Coop said.

"I hate guys like that," Sam said.

"I've noticed," Ben said.

Ben and Sam, Shawn and Coop and Justin were in a circle, sitting in the grass near third base.

"You don't hate guys like that as much as I do," Justin said, eyeballing Pat Seeley. "My dad says it doesn't matter how good you are — or *think* you are — there's a way you're supposed to act."

Pat Seeley moved away from his teammates now, got with his dad, starting doing all these tricky stretches with his dad standing over him.

"The guy acts like there should be a camera watching every move he makes," Ben said.

"There probably is," Coop said, "we just can't see it."

They went back to their own stretching until Ben heard Sam say, "Look out, he's coming over here."

"He must think we missed him," Coop said.

Pat Seeley was as tall as Sam and Justin, long arms and legs, long red hair, freckles.

"How's the little fireballer?" he said to Ben, making no move to shake hands or bump fists.

Ben didn't answer him.

"The way people are talking about you, you must have gotten a lot better at pitching since last year."

"Oh, I'm sorry," Ben said finally. "Were you talking to me, Pat?"

Pat was smiling, but they both knew he didn't mean it. This was part of his act, always had been, Ben was actually surprised it had taken this long for him to make his way across the field.

"Heard you got drilled by *big* fireballer, though, right?"

"Managed to survive," Ben said.

"Barely," Pat Seeley said, "is what I heard. Heard you went through a stretch when you couldn't hit water if you fell out of a boat."

"I'm fine," Ben said.

"Amazing," Coop said.

"What?" Pat Seeley said.

"As much talking as you do, how do you ever have time to listen?"

"Still not funny, Manley," he said.

"Still obnoxious, Seeley," Coop said. Still grinning.

"You talking about me, or yourself?" Pat turned back to Ben. "Better stay loose tonight, I've gotten wild lately." Then he laughed as if he'd said something funny, and said, "Just kidding, I actually have pinpoint control."

"Perfect," Coop said. "Goes with your pinhead!"

"Oh, man, I love listening to your chirp," Pat said. "It's going to make it so much sweeter when we knock you guys out of first place."

Coop started to say something else, but Ben gave him a look, and he swallowed it, just let Pat turn and jog back across the field.

Justin never said a word the whole time Pat was standing there, just glared at him until he left.

"I'd forgotten how much of a jerk that guy is," Justin said.

Ben said, "Hey, you know the deal. The only way to shut up guys like that is by beating them."

Justin looked at Ben and Sam now and said, "At least one of you get on in the first, I don't want to have to wait to get a swing off him."

"He never got over me striking him out to win the championship game a couple of years ago," Ben said. "Remember? They were undefeated until that game."

"Called third strike," Justin said.

"He's been trying to get under my skin ever since," Ben said. "I just don't let him."

"You've got thicker skin than I do," Justin said.

"He's not going to try anything tonight," Ben said. "It's too big a game for them to mess around."

Then Pat Seeley threw the first pitch of the game over Ben's head and put him on the ground.

The ball went over Ben and over the Knights' catcher and over the home plate ump and hit the screen on the fly. When Ben got back up, right away, he saw Pat staring at his right hand, like the ball had slipped, and said, "Man, I am *so* sorry, I was trying to throw the first one *way* too hard."

Then: "You okay?"

Ben didn't say anything to him, just nodded, picked up his bat with his right hand, didn't even make a move to brush dirt off himself.

The ump came up and cleaned home plate. While he did, Ben turned and looked at the Rams' bench. Sam and Coop, Shawn and Justin, were still standing in front of it, staring out at the pitcher's mound.

When Sam looked at Ben, Ben just smiled and mouthed, *I'm fine.*

Got back into the box. Maybe a couple of weeks ago he wouldn't have been fine, wouldn't have wanted to get right back in there. When he couldn't hit the water if he fell out of a boat.

Now he couldn't wait.

"You ready, son?" the ump said.

"Totally," Ben said.

And hit the next pitch he saw so hard up the middle, the ball heading straight at Pat Seeley, it was Pat who ended up on the ground.

When Ben got to first base he thought about calling over to Pat and asking if *he* was okay. But didn't. Wasn't him. Wouldn't ever *be* him. Sometimes Ben McBain thought there were more things he wasn't in sports than he was.

For now he was exactly where he wanted to be:

On first, one-for-one against Pat Seeley, who'd told him to stay loose and hadn't been joking.

Ben stole second, standing up.

Darrelle walked.

Then Sam hit one off the top of the wall in right at Seeley Field, missed a home run by a foot, scoring both Ben and Darrelle, Sam ending up on third with a triple.

Justin now, getting the top-of-the-first swing he wanted off Pat Seeley.

On the first pitch Pat came way inside on Justin, not knocking him down, but forcing him to snap his head back to get out of the way, stumbling back out of the box.

The ump stepped out from behind the plate and said, "Careful now, young man."

Mr. Seeley jumped off the Knights' bench and said, "What, you can't pitch inside in this league?"

Loud as his son. Louder maybe.

In a quiet voice the ump turned and said, "You be careful, too, Coach."

Justin took a strike from Pat, then a ball outside. Then hit the 2-1 pitch *over* the right-field wall, and just like that they had done what Ben said they needed to do, they had shut up Pat Seeley by putting four runs on him before he'd gotten anybody out.

When Justin got back to the bench, got high fives from all of the Rams, Coop said to him, "Oh, that's what Mr. Pinhead meant by his pinpoint control. He puts the ball where J can hit one over the moon."

Ben couldn't help it, he laughed out loud.

When he sat down he saw Pat Seeley staring over at the Rams' bench, his face as red as the rest of him, hair and gloves and bright red shoes.

Somehow Pat settled down after that, went through Shawn and Coop and Kevin Nolti in order, walked slowly back to the Knights' bench, where Ben could see him getting an earful from his father, just the two of them, Pat's dad taking him by the arm and walking him toward right field, talking the whole time, Pat's head down.

Pat struck out the side in the top of the second, then Kevin, starting for the Rams on this night, walked four guys in the bottom of the second, and the Knights got enough clean hits around that to make it 4–2, Rams, going into the top of the third.

Ben leading off.

Before Ben got into the batter's box, he heard Pat say, "You thought that home run was funny?"

"What?" Ben said.

"I wasn't talking to you," Pat said.

Ben shrugged and took his stance and Pat Seeley hit him with the first pitch.

It wasn't his hardest pitch of the night, not the kind of fastball Ben had ripped up the middle, right at him. But it was so far inside that it was actually behind Ben, so that when Ben tried to get out of the way, thinking he had plenty of time, he actually backed into the pitch, which caught him right below his left shoulder.

No doubt in his mind that he'd been hit on purpose, the way there was no doubt in his mind that Pat had buzzed him on purpose when Ben was leading off the game.

Maybe he was dumb enough to think Ben had been laughing at him.

It didn't hurt the way Robbie's pitch had. Didn't hurt at all, actually. Ben didn't even have to go down this time. Just turned and looked at the third-base coaching box, ready to tell Mr. Brown he was fine, to stay where he was, he didn't even want to give Pat Seeley the satisfaction of thinking he needed to be looked at by his coach.

Good thing.

Because he had a perfect look as Justin Bard came running from the Rams' bench before anybody could stop him, came running right at Pat Seeley.

Sam would say later that what happened next was the best first step of Ben's life, that none of them reacted quickly enough when Justin got up, having no idea what he was about to do.

It was Ben who got to him before he crossed the third-base line.

Coop would put it this way, being Coop: "You know how they talk about how fast guys go from home to first? I want to know what your time was from home to *Justin*."

All Ben knew in the moment was that he couldn't let Justin get to Pat. Not sure what the consequences would be if he did. Just knowing they would be bad. Remembering Mr. Brown telling them the first day of practice that their league had a "zero tolerance" policy on fights.

Pat Seeley had nearly hit Ben once already, had come high and inside on Justin, now had hit Ben. And Justin had snapped because of all that.

Or maybe because of everything.

So Ben dropped his bat and flew up the line and launched himself at his own teammate, doing the thing on a Little League ball field that Justin said Ben had never done:

Making a tackle.

Justin ended up on top of Ben, Ben taking the weight of him, feeling the pain of that at the same time but unable to do anything to get out from underneath him before he heard Justin say, "Let me *up*."

Ben thinking he wasn't doing very much to keep him down until he heard Sam say, "No."

It was when Justin rolled off Ben and Ben got up that he saw Sam and Coop pulling Justin to his feet, each with an arm, not so much helping him as holding on to him, walking him back toward the Rams' bench, Mr. Brown and Ben's dad with them now.

All of them making sure he'd gotten as close to the mound as he was going to get.

"What's his *problem*?" Pat Seeley, yelling from the mound, his infielders with him, Pat trying to make it look as if they were holding him back.

Pat Seeley's dad was between the mound and the third-base line by now, Ben noticing his voice was even louder than his son's, pointing at Justin but talking to Mr. Brown, saying, "Can't you control your players?"

Mr. Brown turned when he heard that but didn't respond, walking instead to where the ump was standing, about the spot where Ben had brought down Justin and saying in a calm voice, "What we don't need here is for the adults to make this thing any worse than it already is."

The ump said, "Agreed," and turned to Mr. Seeley and said, "Zip it."

Mr. Seeley acted now as if he'd been hit with a pitch. "Are you talking to me?"

"I am," the ump said.

"Do you know who I am?"

"I do," the ump said. "You're a coach who needs to let me handle this."

Ben walked over to Justin, standing now in front of their bench. Sam and Coop weren't taking any chances, they still each had an arm, like they were about to make a wish. Ben's dad stood between them and the field, while Mr. Brown went to talk to the ump.

"He did that on purpose," Justin said.

He was the one with the red face now.

Ben said, "I know."

"I couldn't take that," Justin said.

Again Ben said, "I know," his voice even quieter than before.

From the mound they could still hear Pat Seeley. "The guy's crazy," he was saying to his teammates, but wanting everybody at Seeley Field to hear him. And maybe people walking their dogs around the duck pond way in the distance.

Sam let go of Justin's arm and started walking toward the field.

"Don't," Ben said. "We're in enough trouble."

"No worries, I won't make more," Sam said. "I just want to tell Pat something."

Ben watched as Sam got as far as the third-base line, then made a time-out signal with his hands, motioning to Pat to come talk to him, like they were boys.

Pat left his teammates and walked over to where Sam was standing, saw Sam talking to him, noticed that Pat Seeley, for what felt like the first time all night, wasn't saying anything.

When Sam was finished, he even gave Pat a nice pat on the shoulder. Boys to the end.

When Sam got back to the bench Ben said, "What did you say to him?"

"Oh, I just told him that if he said one more word to Justin, I was going to make him eat that red glove of his like it was a great big red apple."

Ben couldn't help himself, even with the night having gone crazy. He smiled. "And Pat knew you sort of meant that."

"Oh, yes."

By now there was a conference going on at home plate: The ump, Mr. Brown, Mr. Seeley. Mr. Brown had been doing a lot of the talking, Ben unable to hear him, Mr. Brown's way of speaking as low-key as Sam's was. The only one they could hear was Mr. Seeley, wanting everybody to hear him the way Pat did, demanding that the game be awarded to Kingsland on a forfeit.

174

The Rams' players were all sitting on the bench, Mr. Brown having told them to do that, and not move until he got back.

There were some parents from Rockwell in the stands behind them, Ben already knowing that neither Justin's mom or his dad had made the trip, Shawn's dad was giving Justin a ride home tonight.

Justin was in the middle of the bench, Coop and Ben on one side of him, Sam and Shawn on the other.

"Sometimes I feel like I'm gonna explode," Justin Bard had said in Ben's room that night after he and his mom had come over for dinner.

Tonight he'd exploded.

Finally Mr. Brown finished with the ump and Mr. Seeley. Came back to the Rams and said, "Okay, no forfeit, and the game continues." Paused and said, "Obviously without Justin."

Ben said, "They're not throwing Pat out of the game, too? I told you, Mr. B, he said he saw me laughing at him right before he hit me."

"The ump didn't hear him," Mr. Brown said. "And the ump said that you weren't the one who'd hit the home run off him, there was no reason for him to be throwing at you."

Sam said, "That is so wrong."

"I know," Mr. Brown said. "But it is what it is, and our guy is the one who charged the mound."

They all nodded. Justin just stared, hard, into the dirt in front of the bench, clenching and unclenching his hands.

Mr. Brown said, "Justin gets to stay on the bench, because his parents aren't here. Like I said: We play on. Ben, you get over to first base. And nobody on this team says another word until after we've beaten their butts."

Mr. Brown smiled when he said the last part. It was another time when Ben couldn't believe how much Sam looked like his dad.

"So let's commence doing that," he said.

Ben jogged to first, not going near the mound, going around home plate instead. Darrelle and Sam were getting their bats and helmets. Mr. Brown hadn't gone out to the third-base coach's box just yet, he and Justin were sitting at the end of the bench now, just the two of them, the rest of the guys giving them room, Mr. Brown with his arm around him.

At first base Ben said to his dad, "He might get suspended for the rest of the season, right?"

"Not gonna lie, pal. They take charging the mound *really* seriously in Little League baseball."

"But, Dad, he never got there!"

"Let's worry about that later," he said. "For now, let's focus on winning the game and getting the heck out of here."

Pat Seeley, in what was always going to be his third and last inning, that was the limit, struck out Darrelle and actually had the chops to make a fist as he did.

Sam at the plate now.

And it was clear that Pat wanted no part of him, not after having been told Sam intended to shove his mitt down his throat if he didn't shut up. So Pat threw ball one way outside. Ball two was even more outside.

Ben thought: He's going to intentionally walk him without making it an official intentional walk.

Ben had thought about stealing but didn't want to do anything to distract Sam if he did get a pitch to hit.

Ball three was in the dirt.

Ben just assumed the next pitch wouldn't be anywhere near the strike zone. And it really wasn't, over the plate but up in Sam's eyes.

Ball four until it wasn't, until Sam took a vicious swing and connected and tomahawked the ball over the center-field fence, a screaming line drive from the time it left his bat, Ben watching the flight of the ball and thinking to himself as he did that it might not have been more than ten feet off the ground its whole way out of Seeley Field.

Making the home run that Justin had hit in the top of the first look like a pop fly that had carried.

Ben waited for Sam at home plate, knowing there was no chance, none, zero, that Sam would do anything to show up Pat Seeley, because he never showed up an opponent. Not even this one.

As Ben double-high-fived him he said, "I couldn't tell: You get all of that one?"

"*That* one," Sam said, looking out at the mound, a look there and gone, "was for Justin."

The Rams ended up winning 14–2. Ben pitched the bottom of the sixth. Usually if they had a lead like that Mr. Brown would let Darrelle — who constantly joked that he was a frustrated pitcher — mop up.

But after the fifth, Ben had asked Mr. Brown to please let him finish the game tonight, it was important.

"You got it," Mr. Brown said. "I know I don't have to tell you no funny stuff, that's not you."

One more thing that wasn't Ben.

He went out and struck out the side. The last out was Pat Seeley. Three pitches, nothing close to him, every fastball he threw more unhittable than the one before it. Usually both teams got into lines and shook hands. Not tonight. No gathering for the Rams in the outfield. It was like Ben's dad had said: Win the game, get the heck out of there.

Sam went home with his dad, Justin with Shawn and Mr. O'Brien, Coop with Ben and Ben's dad, the car totally quiet by the time they got to Rockwell, even Coop talked out about Justin and what had happened and what was going to happen to him.

The news the next day was all bad.

And not just because of Justin.

The chairman of the board of Butler County League called Mr. Brown to tell him that Justin had been suspended for the rest of the season, including the playoffs, even though Ben *had* managed to stop him before a fight broke out. The chairman told Sam's dad that it wasn't just Justin going after Pat Seeley the way he did, but that this was a second offense because Justin had already missed a game for throwing his bat.

Two suspensions, same season, they decided he was gone.

The other bad news was something Ben had suspected from the time Justin had landed on him, even though he hadn't mentioned it to anybody.

His left wrist, which had taken most of Justin Bard's weight, the same left wrist that had gotten hit square in the batting cage that day, was swollen to twice its normal size. And way more than after the ball had hit him.

Ben hadn't been suspended from anything, but now he didn't know when he might play again for the Rams.

On the way to Monday's practice Ben was still trying to tell his dad that the wrist felt way better than it looked, honest it did, reminding him that Dr. Freshman said he might only have to miss one game if he was lucky.

Mild sprain, he said, not even close to being the kind of bad ankle sprain that had forced Sam to miss most of the basketball season.

"You heard Doc," Ben said, "if he was really worried about it he would have put me into some kind of soft cast. I'll be good to go when we play Kingsland again on Friday night."

"You didn't think it was worth mentioning when it happened?" his dad said. "So maybe we could have gotten ice on it right away?"

"First of all, there was a lot going on at the time," Ben said. "And second of all, which happens to be *way* more important? I wasn't coming out of that game. Especially not if I was going to get one more chance to face that guy."

They both know which guy he was talking about.

"You know," his dad said, "I was thinking last night that it never changes in sports, that I've been running into kids like Pat Seeley since the time I was a kid. They never think of themselves as being bullies, but they are."

"I think that probably bothered Justin more than anything."

"There's a better way of dealing with bullies, you know that."

"I do," Ben said. "And I know what Justin did was wrong, Dad. But there's just times where you want to smack the other guy. You know I felt that way with Chase during basketball."

"But you *didn't* smack him, or even try," Jeff McBain said. "And I never did no matter how many times I wanted to when I was growing up."

"I get that he broke the rules," Ben said. "But you know it wasn't just Pat who made him act that way last night. It was everything."

"We explained that Justin has been going through a tough time," Ben's dad said.

"The worst."

They were in the parking lot by now, car stopped. Ben's dad turned around and said, "Justin is going to survive this — and that means all of this — you know that, right?"

"I guess."

"Married couples get divorced all the time," Jeff McBain said. "That's just the fact of things. And most of the time when they get divorced there are kids involved, and *all* of the time it's harder on the kids than anybody else. But the beauty of children, and trust me, I'm a trained professional, is how resilient you guys are. So the children of divorce get through it. Justin will get through it, the way he'll get through missing these games."

"I know you're right, Dad," Ben said. "I just feel like they're not seeing the whole picture, is all."

"They're probably not," Jeff McBain said. "Sam's dad and I plan to have one more conversation with Ed Goodman — he's the chairman of the baseball board — at the end of the week, take another run at him."

"So you're not giving up?"

"I'm a McBain," his dad said. "Where do you think you get that from?"

Ben missed the second Moreland game, which the Rams lost, dropping them into a second-place tie with Darby, Parkerville right behind them, the Moreland Tigers going into first place by themselves, everybody with one last game before the play-offs started.

The Rams' last regular season game would be against Kingsland on Friday night at Highland Park. The playoffs would start Saturday. If the Rams beat Kingsland — it would mean beating Pat Seeley again — the worst they could do was finish in second place, which meant their first playoff game would be at home.

But that wasn't the big baseball news of the week for their team, at least not as far as Ben was concerned. The big news was that Sam's dad was scheduled to go over to Darby on

Wednesday and plead Justin's case one last time in front of Mr. Goodman, this year's board chairman for Butler County baseball.

"You think Mr. Brown will be able to change this guy's mind?" Lily said to Ben.

They weren't in the swings at McBain Field on this night. Just the two of them sitting on the front steps of Ben's house after dinner, Ben having invited Lily over to eat with him and his parents.

Before that, Dr. Freshman had declared Ben good to go for the playoffs, telling him it wouldn't be the worst thing in the world for him to take one more game off, just to be on the safe side.

"I don't know Mr. Goodman," Ben said. "Dad says he used to coach in the league when his son still played. But you know how it is with grown-ups once they make up their minds about something."

"Does Mr. Goodman know about Justin's mom and dad, and about him moving?"

"Dad says he does, the whole board does."

"And that doesn't count for anything?"

"Guess not, Lils," Ben said, and then he said, "This *stinks.*"

"You did everything you could, McBain," she said. Poked him in the arm and said, "I hear your tackle could have made SportsCenter."

"That's supposed to make me feel good?"

He turned and saw her smiling at him. "You're with me," she said. "So it's not like you're going to feel bad."

"Excellent point."

They were both finishing off ice-cream cones.

"You gotta remember something," she said. "Just because Justin's season is over doesn't mean yours is."

"I'm not an idiot."

"Occasionally," she said.

"Another excellent point."

"You guys can still win, and that would mean you won in football and baseball this year and would've won in basketball if Sam hadn't gotten hurt."

"I know all that, Lils. And after the way the season started for me, it would be an awesome thing to win the championship, make it an awesome season. It's just that . . ."

"It's just that it was Justin's season, too."

"Yeah," he said, turned to her again, saw that she was still smiling as she wiped some ice cream from the corner of his mouth, like that was the most natural thing in the world for her to do.

Quiet now on his street. Just the first night sound of crickets. A dog barking a few houses up. Ben thought: This should have felt like the best week of the whole summer. His wrist had healed — again — and the playoffs were starting and the Rams were right there.

But it didn't feel that way.

"He's such a good guy."

"Justin?" Lily said.

"You know what I keep thinking about, Lils? With everything that was happening to him, he didn't have to help me when I was, like, totally lost at the plate. There was nothing in it for him, we were friends but not that kind of friends. But he did it, anyway."

"Look who's talking."

"We always talk about how there's nothing more important to us than being a good friend and then he hauled off and turned out to be a *great* friend I didn't even knew I had." Ben shook his head, hard. "I know *what* he did should cost him. I get that. But who he is should count for something, too."

"When you're right, you're right, McBain."

"It just doesn't do me any good or Justin any good."

Lily stood up.

"Let's take a walk to the swings before I have to go home."

"Why?"

"Because I might have an idea."

"You can't have your idea here?"

"I have better ideas at the swings," she said.

So the two of them walked across McBain Field in the gray light you got in summer right before it got dark. He didn't say anything and Lily didn't say anything until they sat down. They always sat in the same swings, as long as Ben could remember, Lily on his right.

Finally she said, "Grown-ups always think they understand kids, because they were kids once themselves. But their problem, McBain, is that they think that we think the way they did when they were our age."

She wasn't done yet and he knew it, there were times

when she was thinking out loud like this when Ben knew to just shut up and let her keep thinking.

"But they don't think like us, no matter how hard they try, because it was so long ago they don't remember what the heck they were thinking about."

Ben saw her nodding and smiling, brightening this little piece of the gray light.

Now she turned to look right at him as she said, "You need to tell Mr. Goodman about Justin."

"Me."

"*You,*" she said. "Not Sam's dad and not even your dad. You."

"No way."

"Way," Lily said. "You say that Mr. Goodman needs to know who Justin is. You know better than anybody now. So you tell him."

And he did.

Mr. Brown agreed with Lily.

Told Ben he didn't just like the idea, that he loved it.

"Tell Lily she's a genius," Mr. Brown said.

And Ben laughed and said, "I'd rather not, if that's okay with you."

Now it was the next afternoon and Mr. Brown was driving them both to Mr. Goodman's law office in Darby. They'd decided that Mr. Brown should still sit in on the meeting, but that it would be Ben who did the talking about Justin Bard.

"I'm always telling people that you and Sam know way more about sports than I do," Mr. Brown said. "I should have figured you probably know more about lots of things."

"I still think I'm out of my league," Ben said.

"You just tell Ed Goodman what you told Lily and what you told me," Sam's dad said. "And maybe you can get Justin back in *our* league."

"Mr. Goodman would have to be a lawyer," Ben said.

"But he's a dad, too. And you know he used to coach."

"What if I totally mess this up?"

Mr. Brown said to him, "You've never thought that way going into a big game in your life. Don't start now."

Ed Goodman was a big man who looked to Ben as if he would have made a better football coach than a baseball coach, wearing a white shirt and tie, sitting behind a desk that seemed to take up about half an office looking out over Main Street in Darby.

When everybody was seated Mr. Goodman said to Ben, "I saw that shot you hit to spoil our kids' unbeaten season in basketball. Still don't know how you got it over the Braggs boy."

"Neither do I, sir."

"We've got a saying in Rockwell," Mr. Brown said, "about how amazing it is that good teams seem to keep following Ben around."

Mr. Goodman smiled now, leaned forward, clasped his big hands together, and said, "I want you to know, son, I like being a lawyer a lot better than I like being a judge in a case like this. Or jury. But having said that, I very much want to hear what you have to say about young Mr. Bard."

Ben swallowed, but it didn't help, his mouth felt as dry as the papers on the desk between him and Mr. Goodman. He thought about asking for some water, but he was ready to go right now, and didn't want to lose his nerve. He kept telling himself that was the same as reading one of his essays in front of the class, what his English teacher called "declamations," from memory.

He'd spent all last night practicing what he wanted to say to Mr. Goodman the way he practiced those.

He started by telling Mr. Goodman that he knew the rules about fighting, that they all did, Justin included, he wasn't going to act as if Justin hadn't done something wrong by trying to charge Pat Seeley. He knew nothing good could ever come out of a fight, even one that didn't actually happen, he'd found out himself when Justin had landed on his wrist.

"My dad has always told me that the only thing fighting proves is who's the better fighter," Ben said, "and that you usually know that beforehand."

"Smart man, your dad."

"We all know that Justin would've won a fight with Pat Seeley," Ben said, "but that doesn't matter now. What *matters* is that Justin has *lost* the rest of the season."

Mr. Goodman smiled again. "From what I know of the Seeley boy — and his father — I can see why you all would have enjoyed watching the whole thing play out. But we both know that would've been wrong. For everybody. Same as charging the mound is wrong. And believe me, Ben, no one feels worse about this than I do, and the other board members, all of whom are dads. We all know how valuable these seasons are."

Ben took a deep breath. "I'm not sure you do, sir. Not in Justin's case."

"I'm aware of his family situation."

"But that's the thing, Mr. Goodman. His family situation, like you call it, is just a part of this. I know he'll have other seasons when he moves to Cameron. But he's never going to have this season. He's never going to know what would've

189

happened if he'd been with *us*. The only season that matters is the one you're playing."

Ben leaned forward. "My dad has another big thing about sports. He's always telling me to appreciate these seasons because nobody ever knows how many they're going to have. But what Justin knows now is that he's never going to have another one with his friends here. And now it's over. And I don't think it should end the way it did."

Ben stopped, because he was out of breath, the only sounds in the room in that moment, other than the ticking of a big stand-up clock against the wall to his right, and the sound of his own breathing.

Mr. Goodman said, "Your coach here says that you know something about Justin that nobody else on the team does. Something he did for you."

Ben told him then about getting hit by Robbie Burnett. And how it made him afraid of the ball. And about the day at Highland Park when Justin had gotten Ben turned around.

"That's who he is, Mr. Goodman. He's way more than the hothead who *lost* his head because Pat Seeley was acting like a total loser. Or somebody who's been mad at the world all season because of his mom and dad and moving away." Swallowed again, kept going. "People always want to talk about my heart. But I don't have any idea how I'd handle what he's going through. And if I *was* going through what he is? I don't know that I would have found the time to help some-body else through something."

In a quiet voice Mr. Brown said, "I do."

"You're a good friend," Mr. Goodman said to Ben.

"So is Justin."

"You understand the position I'm in, Ben, because the law of the league is so clear."

"But is that the spirit of the law, Mr. Goodman?"

"That come from your dad, too?"

Ben nodded.

"I wish my son listened to me the way you obviously listen to your father."

"Justin will never even think about fighting ever again," Ben said. "He didn't even fight the other night! It's crazy when you think about it, losing this much over a fight he didn't even have. I know I sound like I'm stuck on that. But it's true."

"He has lost a lot," Mr. Goodman said. His voice quiet now. "And is losing a lot. No one knows that better than I do, my parents got divorced when I was a couple of years younger than Justin is now."

"Justin's mom told me one night that she's moving out of Rockwell because there's too many memories for her there," Ben said. "I just don't want Justin's last memory with us in baseball to be what happened the other night."

Mr. Goodman stood up now, came around his desk. Ben and Mr. Brown stood up. Mr. Goodman shook Ben's hand again, Ben making sure to look him in the eye the way he'd been taught, even if it meant craning his neck back to do it.

"You've given me some things to think about," Mr. Goodman said.

"Thanks for listening to a kid," Ben said.

Ed Goodman looked over at Mr. Brown and said, "Some kid."

"Tell me about it," Sam's dad said.

Then Ed Goodman looked down at Ben and said, "Now I understand how you made that shot."

"If you don't take the shot," Ben said, "you'll never know whether it would have gone in or not."

"That one more thing from your dad?"

Ben was the one smiling now as he said, "No, I came up with that one myself."

Ben's mom answered the phone right before dinner and said that his coach wanted to talk to him.

When she handed the receiver over to him Ben covered the mouthpiece and said, "Did he say anything?"

Beth McBain said, "Yes."

"What?"

"He said he wanted to talk to you."

"Funny, Mom."

"I know," she said.

"Hey, Mr. Brown," he said into the phone.

Mr. Brown said, "I didn't even tell Sam yet, he's not home from Coop's even though he's supposed to be. But what I wanted you to hear this first."

"Mr. Goodman said no, didn't he?"

"No," Mr. Brown said. "He said yes."

"Yes!"

"The deal is this," Sam's dad said, "Justin serves out the rest of his suspension with the Kingsland game tomorrow night. And he has to apologize to Pat Seeley. But he gets to play in the playoffs."

"He's got to apologize to a guy who started out the game buzzing Justin and me and then hit me on purpose?" Ben said. "A guy Justin never touched?"

"Part of the deal," Mr. Brown said. "And just so you know? According to Ed Goodman, Pat Seeley's dad screamed louder about this than he did when he was screaming for a forfeit the other night. If that makes you feel any better."

"It kind of does, actually."

"Thought it might." There was a pause at the other end of the phone and then Sam's dad said, "Why don't you be the one to give Justin the good news."

"It's your team, Mr. B."

"But this is your show, even though I bet you didn't even tell him you spoke to Ed Goodman, did you?"

"No," Ben said. "I didn't want him to get his hopes up. I felt like I was throwing that Hail Mary to Sam all over again."

"You going to tell him?"

"Nah," Ben said. "Maybe later?"

"Or maybe never?"

"Maybe," Ben said. "I just figure that we're even now. In a way, he did for me what I did for him: Helped give him his season back."

"But you'll call him?"

"Think I might go tell Justin in person, just to see the look on his face."

Ben hung up the phone, turned around, saw both of his parents standing there, his dad's arm around his mom's shoulders, both of them smiling at him.

Beth McBain said, "I gather you have to be somewhere?"

"You guys go ahead and eat," Ben said.

His dad said that now that he thought about it, he wasn't all that hungry right now, and offered to drive Ben over to Justin's house.

Ben said he'd rather ride his bike, if that was okay with them.

"Let the moment last a little bit?" his dad said.

"Something like that," Ben said.

"What did you tell Ed Goodman?"

Ben shrugged. "Just a bunch of stuff that you keep telling me."

Ben asked the guard at the gate if it was all right if he surprised Justin Bard, he had some great news for him. Gave the man his name and said he and Justin played on the same baseball team.

"Nice boy, that boy," the guard said. "Gonna miss him."

"Me, too."

"You go on ahead."

Maybe it was because of the way the day had gone, the news Mr. Brown had just given him and he was about to give to Justin, but Ben started to imagine he'd get to the bottom of Justin's driveway and the "For Sale" sign would be gone, that Justin's mom had decided to stay in Rockwell, they weren't moving after all.

But the sign was right where it was the first time Ben had seen it.

Only one happy ending today.

He rode his bike up the driveway, set it down near the front porch, rang the doorbell, Mrs. Bard opened the door, took one look at him, and said, "You look like you're about to pop, Ben McBain."

Ben lowered his voice to a whisper, not knowing if Justin was anywhere near them.

"The league changed its mind, Mrs. Bard. Justin can play in the playoffs."

"You are kidding!" she said, and came out on the porch, closing the door behind her.

"How?" she said. "Why?"

"I guess they looked at all the facts and decided it was the right thing to do."

"He's been so down," she said. "Worse than he already was. This feels like a small miracle."

Ben said, "Like some crazy shot in basketball that went in."

She said Justin was in his room. Ben took the stairs two at a time, knocked on the closed door, didn't wait for an answer, walked in, and saw Justin on his bed, headphones on, watching something on his laptop.

"You can play!" Ben said.

Justin took off his headphones and said, "What did you just say?"

"I said you can play on Saturday!" Ben said.

"Don't mess me with me."

"Not messing with you," Ben said. "Your suspension ends with the Kingsland game."

"Who says?"

"Mr. Brown says. And Mr. Goodman, the chairman of the league."

Ben told him the rest of the deal then, about apologizing to Pat Seeley for rushing him the way he did. Ben was thinking Justin might explode when he heard that, but he just grinned.

"You're cool with that?" Ben said.

"Totally."

"For real?"

"Coop's the one always saying he can fake sincerity when he has to, right?"

"One of his favorite lines."

"Well, if he can do it I can do it."

"I won't tell him you said it exactly like that," Ben said. "He thinks it's like a move he invented."

"So we all get to play at least one more game together?" Justin said.

"Maybe more than that if we keep winning," Ben said. "Maybe we keep playing all the way through the states."

"I'm good with that."

"Me, too," Justin said.

Then he closed his laptop, reached over, and placed his headphones on his nightstand, stood up on his bed.

And then started jumping for joy.

Pat Seeley didn't even show up with the rest of the Kingsland team on Friday night, his dad informing Mr. Brown before the game that his son had a "tired" arm and that there was no reason to risk injury since the Knights had no chance of making the playoffs.

"Tired arm?" Coop said. "More like he's tired of us beating his butt."

"Sure hope he feels better by next season," Sam said. "A good guy like that."

"That's the only bad part of this," Ben said. "That we don't get to face him again until next season."

"And it'll be a total shame not seeing those red shoes again," Coop said. "They reminded me a little bit of Dorothy's in *The Wizard of Oz*."

Because Pat Seeley wasn't there, Justin came and apologized to Mr. Seeley instead, saying he was sorry for everything that had happened that night.

Ben and the guys had walked over with Justin, just as a way of showing that they had his back, so they all heard Pat

Seeley's dad say, "I'm not going to lie to you, son, I think you got off easy."

Justin let that go. Mr. Brown didn't. He said, "You ever wonder why your son acts the way he does, Coach?"

Then turned and led the Rams back to their bench, where Coop said to him, "You see the look on his face? He looked like he'd swallowed a bug."

The Rams won, 8–4, locking up the second seed for the playoffs, setting up a home game against Darby on Saturday night at Highland Park, Sam against Chase Braggs, Sam pitching three no-hit innings to start, the Rams finally winning 4–1, Justin knocking in three of the runs with a double and a single, Ben pitching the top of the sixth, striking out Ryan Hurley, their best hitter, with two on to end it.

In the other semifinal Parkerville, which had ended up with the fourth seed, upset Moreland, which meant that the Rams' season would end the way it had begun, them against Robbie Burnett, at home, on Sunday night.

Maybe the way it was supposed to end.

Ben looking for the best possible ending, for him and the team and for Justin, maybe Justin most of all.

One more night together for all of them at Highland Park.

But when the night came, Parkerville jumped out to a 10–0 lead. After just the third inning. At which point Coop would say, "It's a good thing they don't have the slaughter rule in a championship game or the season would be over already."

*   *   *

The Parkerville coach had gambled, deciding to save Robbie for the championship game, gambling — it paid off — that they could find a way to beat Moreland with their other best starting pitcher, a kid named Jeff DiVeronica, who had still been recovering from an ankle he'd broken in soccer at the start of the season.

Mr. Brown had gone with Sam against Darby in the semis because it was Sam's turn to pitch, saying that he wasn't going to change the way he'd been doing things all season, saying that he trusted Shawn — their number two starter — to beat Parkerville as much as he would have trusted him to beat Darby.

Only Shawn had nothing on this night. Less than nothing, really, no control, no fastball. He walked the first two guys in the top of the first, gave up a solid hit after that, scored Parkerville's first run, then gave up a homer to Robbie. By the time Shawn got the third out, a couple of guys still on, it was 5–0 and Parkerville had batted around.

When they got to the bench Mr. Brown told them to gather around him, fast.

"Listen, they hit, now we hit," he said. "We can't do anything about what just happened, and we don't have to come all the way back the first time we bat. We just do what we do. We play. Which means forgetting the top of the first, because I have already."

"I haven't," Shawn said in a quiet voice.

"Well, I'm telling you to," Mr. Brown said. "We've got six innings to make up five runs. We've scored five runs in games plenty of times this season, and now we're going to do it again. Okay?"

He looked around, trying to go from face to face as quickly as he could.

Ben finally spoke, saying, "Let's go get a couple back right now," then went to get his helmet and his bat, thinking to himself that there was a lot more going on right now than just facing Robbie Burnett again.

Thinking that the most important thing in the world right now felt like getting on base any way he could, he didn't care who was pitching, it could have been Lily Wyatt.

He singled to right on a 2-2 pitch, no fear, watching the ball the way Justin had retaught him to do that, going with an out-side pitch, taking it the other way like you were supposed to. But Darrelle struck out, Sam lined out to short, a screamer. Two out. Justin seemed to have gotten all of the first pitch Robbie threw him, Ben thinking it might be 5–2 when the ball came down, but he caught it a little too much up the bat and the right fielder caught the ball about ten feet in front of the fence, inning over, game still 5–0.

It was 8–0 in the top of the second, Shawn still in there, seeming to have settled down. But then Justin booted a routine ball with two outs and Darrelle threw wild on a routine grounder to *him*. Then John McQuaid, Parkerville's first base-man, hit one about a foot fair over the left-field fence and Mr. Brown had to come out and replace Shawn with Kevin Nolti.

Ben was standing on the mound, waiting for Kevin to jog in from left field to take his warm-ups.

Justin was there with him and Darrelle. And Mr. Brown.

"If they can score eight, we can score eight, I still believe that," Sam's dad said.

But in that moment Ben wasn't sure he believed, just watched as he rubbed up the new ball and handed it to Kevin and said, "Just keep it at 8–0, Kev." Grinning as he added, "I'll pay you."

Kevin got a strikeout to end the Parkerville half of the inning. But then Robbie struck out the side in the second and when Darrelle made a two-out error in the third with guys running from second and third, it was 10–0 and Coop was talking about the slaughter rule.

All of them looking at the scoreboard, knowing what was up there, still not believing their eyes.

Sam said to Ben, "We've never lost like this in anything."

"And now we're losing a championship game like this."

"Robbie comes out after three," Sam said. "Even if he pitches one more inning like he's been pitching, that still gives us three innings to catch up."

"That's your plan?" Ben said.

"I wouldn't call it a plan, exactly," Sam said. "Think of it as an early Christmas list."

Ben said, "This isn't the way the season was supposed to end, you know that, right?"

"Remember what the old ain't-over-till-it's-over dude said about that," Sam said. "Let's just see if we can cut this sucker in half and go from there."

"Now *that* sounds like a plan," Ben said.

They bumped fists.

They didn't score off Robbie in the third, he went through the bottom of the order one-two-three, working fast, striking out two, looking as if he could pitch this way all night if he had to. Kevin held Parkerville in the top of the fourth. Ben leading off the bottom of the fourth.

"You guys get on and this time I won't miss my pitch," Justin said at the bat rack.

Ben nodded.

Justin said, "Way too much happened this season for *this* to happen now."

"I'll do my job," he said. "I know Sam will. Then you do yours. Let's at least let those guys know we're still here."

John McQuaid pitching for Parkerville now. Ben hit the second pitch he saw from him up the middle for a single. Darrelle worked John for a walk, fouling off three pitches at 3-2 before he did. Then John made a great first pitch to Sam, the ball running in on him, Sam barely managing to get his bat on the ball, rolling it toward third base.

But the ball died in the grass in front of their third baseman like a perfect bunt, the kid knew enough not to throw the ball, not with Sam running.

Bases loaded, nobody out, Justin at the plate.

The kid who wasn't even supposed to have been in this game trying to get the Rams back into the game.

Ben standing at third base and not thinking like a base runner, thinking like a pitcher.

Thinking: John McQuaid ought to walk him, even with the bases loaded.

Thinking: The scoreboard would look a lot better at 10–1

than it would if Justin did what he'd promised he was going to do if he got his pitch again.

And Ben thought Justin had missed his pitch when the count was 2-2, John throwing him a please-crush-me fastball that Justin fouled back, Ben thinking that might be the most hittable pitch Justin was going to see.

But if there was one thing Ben knew about Justin by now it was that he had no fear at the plate. Especially had no fear hitting with two strikes, the way a lot of kids in their league did. The way a lot of hitters did, period, all the way to the big leagues.

Even with two strikes on him, he wouldn't give in to the pitcher, didn't give in when John McQuaid threw him a ball that was just high, bringing so many loud groans from the Parkerville infielders and from their bench guys that the home plate ump called time, took off his mask, came in front of the plate, pointed at the infield, and then the bench and said, "Lose the sound effects. *Now.*"

Justin never moved, didn't step out. Just waited. Looking perfectly calm. Like the scoreboard didn't matter, the runners on the bases in front of him didn't matter.

Like the whole season was just him and John McQuaid and the space between them.

Ben watching and thinking all over again that John should be the one to give in, and throw ball four.

He went right at him instead.

Justin didn't miss.

As soon as Ben saw the ball come off his bat and heard

the sound of the ball coming off his bat — a sound only his bat made, at least in their league — Ben knew it was gone. Stood halfway between third and home just to watch the ball clear the right-field fence this time, by a lot, the only word in his head one of Coop's favorite words in the English language:

Gorgeous.

Parkerville 10 now, Rockwell 4.

They made sure not to do any celebrating at home plate, still down six. Ben and Darrelle and Sam just waited for Justin to slam his right foot down on the plate, all of them giving him high fives, Justin not even changing his expression as he led them back to the guys waiting for him in front of their bench.

All he said to his teammates was, "Game on."

"Lot better than off," Cooper Manley said.

Still six runs down, six outs away from their season being over if they didn't do something about that, and right now.

But the game was *on*.

They could all feel it now, on the bench, in the field, there was even more noise from the bleachers now on the first base side, the home side, of Highland Park.

Kevin Nolti held Parkerville again in the top of the fifth, Kevin pitching better than he had all year in the moment when they needed him to do that.

Ben was due up second in the bottom of the fifth, but while John McQuaid, still in there for Parkerville, was warming up, Ben was the one gathering his teammates around him.

"You guys ever hear of that Petaluma, California, team in the Little League World Series?" he said. "From a couple of years ago?"

"I do," Justin said. "Saw the game on ESPN."

"So you know what they did."

"They came all the way back from 10–0 down," he said. "One of the greatest Little League games I ever saw."

Ben was hoping that Justin wouldn't tell the rest of it, that they came all the way back and tied the game before losing in the end.

But he didn't.

"You know what happened to those guys after they were down ten–zip?" Ben said. "They ended up riding in a parade through the Main Street of their town."

True, that's what happened when they got back from Williamsport.

Ben said, "It's because they didn't stop playing when the scoreboard told them the game was over."

"Anybody feel like quitting here?" Sam said.

They all shook their heads.

"More runs," Coop said, like he was asking for more ice cream.

"Let's do this," Justin said.

Ben singled with one out, third hit of the game, Robbie Burnett — out in left now — having to make a sliding stop to keep the ball from rolling to the wall. Darrelle singled Ben to third, Sam doubled them both home.

And now it was 10–6.

Sam went to third on a wild pitch. Justin hit another rocket, this one to center, but to the deepest part of Highland Park, their center fielder having plenty of time to go back on it, plenty of room to catch it.

Sac fly. Sam could have walked home.

Parkerville 10, Rockwell 7.

Shawn singled, so did Coop, Kevin walked. But then Michael Clayton struck out with the bases loaded to end the inning. The Rams still got a huge cheer from their fans. Ben turned and saw they were all standing now, all the parents, including Justin's. Lily was there, too, with Ben's mom.

Ben getting the ball now, down three runs, knowing he had to keep the Parkerville lead right there, hold them at ten runs the way Kevin Nolti had as they started — fought — to come back.

"Just pitch like the game is tied," Mr. Brown said to Ben.

"Nah," Ben said. "I'm going to pitch like we're a run ahead, the way we're gonna be in a few minutes."

He got the bottom of the order, Kevin having pitched through Robbie and John McQuaid and the middle of their order in the fifth. Ben struck out the first two guys, popped up their right fielder for the third out.

And just like that it was the bottom of the last at Highland Park, unless they tied the thing and sent it into extra innings.

Just like that it might be the bottom of the season.

The Rams playing just to keep playing now.

Still down three.

Wasn't the season that had started with Ben getting hit in

the arm and losing his confidence as if he'd really been hit in the *heart*. Wasn't the season of Justin's thrown bat or him going after Pat Seeley before Ben made his flying tackle.

Wasn't the season of any of that.

Just the bottom of the sixth at Highland Park. Going into it with a chance after being ten runs behind.

Sam came over to Ben on the bench, Ben scheduled to be third man up.

"We win this thing," Sam said, "it would go with anything we've ever done together."

"Yeah, it would."

"Let's do this," Sam said.

Ben smiled at his friend. A friend as cool as Lily was. Which meant nobody cooler. "You always say that," Ben said.

"But I really *really* mean it this time."

Then there were two ridiculously fast outs by the third Parkerville pitcher of the game, one of their best basketball players, Matt Sample, who'd been playing third base before this. Robbie had told them before the game he'd become their closer since the last time they'd played the Rams.

Just like that they were down to their last out. Ben started to walk from the on-deck area toward the plate when he felt a hand on his arm, startling him, he was that zoned out about not making the last out of the season.

Justin.

Putting his hand out so Ben could shake it.

"Whatever happens, I wouldn't have missed this game for anything," he said.

"It's not over yet."

"You got me one more game," Justin said. "Get me one more swing."

Matt Sample, overthrowing, trying to end it, trying to win the championship for Parkerville, came inside with his first pitch.

Way inside.

Ben didn't even move his feet to get out of the way, just did his Jeter lean-back, like he was sucking in his belly.

Only afraid of the season being over, nothing else.

Took a ball outside. Then a strike. Two and one. Ben felt that if he was going to see a good pitch he was going to see it now, Matt Sample not wanting to fall behind more than he was, certainly not wanting to give Ben a walk with two outs and nobody on and the championship trophy so close he probably felt like he could feel it already.

Put Ben on and then he had to get Darrelle or risk having to face Sam, and everybody on the Parkerville team had seen the way Sam had hit the ball tonight.

Matt Sample had to want Ben to put the ball in play, because maybe he'd hit the ball right at somebody and the game would be over.

The way Ben would have been thinking if he were trying to close this game out before the Rams got any closer than they already were.

Matt threw a fastball over the plate, about knee-high, and Ben went down and got it and drove it over the shortstop's head, Robbie charging and playing it on one hop.

Season not over.

Not yet.

"I wasn't making the last out of the stinking season," Ben said to his dad at first base, just loud enough for him to hear, almost whispering.

"Would have bet everything in my wallet that you wouldn't," his dad said.

Then he said, "Remember what I told you about the Sox in '04."

His dad, a Boston College guy, was a Red Sox fan, and had always told Ben about the ninth inning of Game 4 of the 2004 American League Championship Series. Red Sox three outs away from being swept by the Yankees. Mariano Rivera, greatest closer of them all, coming in to get those three outs. Rivera: Part of the Yankees' Core Four.

What happened next was a walk, a stolen base, a single up the middle. Game tied. The Red Sox won that one in extra innings, Ben knew, and won the next night in extra innings and finally won the series in seven games. Greatest comeback in baseball history, first time a team had come back from three games to none down.

"Biggest baseball story of all time," his dad always said, "and it started with a walk, a stolen base, a single up the middle."

We don't need to win four games, Ben thought, just one.

But they still needed runs to make this the greatest comeback in the only history that mattered to them:

Their own.

Ben's eyes locked on Sam's in the on-deck circle. And saw Sam smile and hold up one finger.

Meaning one more base runner and then he had his chance to keep the season going.

Darrelle Clayton swung at the first pitch Matt Sample threw him, hit this little blooper toward short right field, Ben not having time to see if John McQuaid, back at first, had time to go back and catch it, Ben running all the way with two outs.

But as he rounded second he looked over his shoulder and saw the ball falling, somehow finding a patch of grass even though John was there, their right fielder, their second baseman.

Ben made third easily, Darrelle stopped at first.

Two on, two out. Somehow, after 10–0, Sam Brown was the potential tying run at the plate. And if Ben knew — *knew* — he wasn't going to make the last out of the season, he knew Sam wasn't going to do that, either.

Ben would have bet the money in everybody's wallets on that.

The Parkerville coach called time, jogged out to the mound to talk to Matt Sample, Ben watching Matt, watching as he nodded his head, the coach doing all the talking.

And what they had to be talking about was throwing strikes, not walking Sam Brown, not with Justin Bard in the on-deck circle, not after he'd already hit one grand slam tonight.

Justin wouldn't just be the potential winning run at that point.

He'd be the championship run.

Their coach jogged back to their bench on the third-base side. Matt Sample against Sam now. Matt tried to get ahead, thinking — hoping? — Sam might take a strike, might be looking for a walk with Justin coming up behind him.

Sam took a strike all right.

Took it up the gap in right-center, took it past the center fielder and past the right fielder and, by the time everybody had stopped running, Ben had scored and Darrelle had scored from first and Sam Brown was on third and it was 10–9 at Highland Park.

Justin Bard coming to the plate.

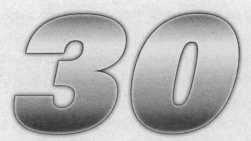

They would be able to watch the way the game ended later, it turned out that Sam's mom had started recording the game after Justin's grand slam started to bring them back. Started to make it a game.

"I had a feeling something special might be happening," she said later, at which point Sam's dad said, "As usual, you were right, dear."

Mrs. Brown patted him on the arm and said, "You can never go wrong saying that."

But Ben didn't need the video from Sam's mom to remember what happened. By now, because he loved sports the way he did, he knew you never needed video when something great happened, whether it happened in the game you were playing or the game you were watching.

The best plays and the best moments, they got burned into your memory, and sometimes your heart, and you knew you'd never forget them.

What happened at the end of the championship game, Justin at the plate, Sam on third, Rams still down a run:

Justin took a ball and then a strike at the knees from Matt Sample. Then another ball, this one at least a foot outside. Ben thinking that Matt might be the Parkerville pitcher to pitch around Justin and take his chances with Shawn. Make this into one of those unintentional intentional walks the announcers talked about sometimes, not giving Justin anything to hit, hoping he might chase a bad pitch and get himself out.

The next pitch was outside, too.

Just not far enough to prevent Justin Bard from giving it a ride.

There was no yelling on the bench when they heard the sound of his bat on this one — *that* sound, again — because they were all too nervous. But the Rams all stood up and watched the flight of the ball, toward deep left-center.

"Get out," Coop said to Ben. "*Get . . . out.*"

Parkerville's center fielder started to chase and then stopped, like he knew there was no chance for him to chase the ball down even if it stayed in the ballpark.

The only movement in the outfield was Robbie Burnett, a streak, running full-out to his left, Robbie having gotten a great jump as soon as he saw the ball come off Justin's bat.

Only guy at Highland Park thinking he had a chance to *keep* the ball in the park and save a game his team had been winning since 10–0 and was still winning now.

For now.

"*Get . . . out . . . of . . . here . . . please,*" Coop said.

Now his voice was rising.

"He got enough," Ben said, pounding his fist into the back of Coop's shoulder.

Robbie Burnett was still the only one who didn't think so, not even slowing up now as he got close to the four-foot wall in left-center, running at full speed, glove up in the air like he was a receiver trying to catch the kind of sweet long pass Robbie could throw in football.

Coaches always talked about how they wanted guys willing to run through a wall. Robbie Burnett looked like he was ready to do just that, still tracking the ball Justin had hit the whole time.

Kept running like that, glove still held high, until he hit the wall.

And then disappeared over it.

The cheers from the Rams' side of Highland Park disappearing with him, as if somebody had turned off all the sound that had come out of their bleachers once Justin had connected the way he had.

Now the Parkerville short stop, Alex Gomez, was running toward the wall, to the plate where Robbie Burnett had gone over it, so was the umpire who'd been behind second base.

Ben saw Sam standing and watching it all from home plate.

Justin was halfway between second and third, dead stop, staring out there along with everybody else.

Coop was the only one speaking. Of course. "When I said 'get out,'" he said, "I *didn't* mean Robbie."

Robbie hitting the wall harder than he'd hit Ben with that pitch, something that now felt as if it had happened in another summer.

They saw his glove then.

Saw the glove and then they saw Robbie Burnett reaching

into his glove, taking the ball out of it, showing it to the ump, holding the ball as high as he could.

Saw the ump turn and put his right arm high and let everybody know that Robbie had made the greatest catch any of them would probably ever see. Let them know that the game was over and the Rams' season was over.

That it was still 10–9 Parkerville, the way it would always be.

The Rams got into the line between the mound and home plate, none of them saying anything to each other, just saying "Good game" to the Parkerville players, one after another. Ben was last in the line, as usual.

Robbie was at the back of the Parkerville line.

Ben smiled at him, up-topped him with a high five, said, "How did you make that catch?"

Robbie said, "How did you make that throw to Sam in football?"

"You okay?" Ben said.

"I can take a hit," he said. "Just like you."

"See you in football," Ben said.

Mr. Brown went out on the field, brought Ben and Sam and Justin with him, collected the runner-up trophy, came back, and told the team that he'd never been prouder to finish second his whole life.

Then they all watched from the bench as Robbie and the Parkerville players knelt in front of the mound, the championship in the grass in front of them, and posed for pictures.

The trophy that Ben was sure was going to belong to them, all the way until Justin's ball came down and Robbie's glove came up.

In a quiet voice Sam said to Ben, "It would have been *so* awesome."

And Ben said, "It *was* awesome."

"That why I don't feel as crushed as I should?"

"Yeah," Ben said, then said to Sam Brown, "This game tonight, the way we came back? This is why we play."

About fifteen minutes later, as the rest of the Rams were having their snacks, no one in any hurry to leave the field, Ben broke off from his teammates, walked across the infield and into the outfield, walked all the way out, opened the door in center, walked to his left, to the place where Robbie had landed, thought about what he must have felt like when he felt the ball in the pocket of his glove.

Then he leaned his arms on the top of the fence and looked back at the field.

At his own teammates, eating away and drinking and talking and already laughing; it was what you did when you were eleven, he knew, maybe that's why Coop wanted to stay eleven forever.

Looked at the Parkerville players, still celebrating, still posing for pictures for the parents holding up their camera phones.

Saw Justin's parents, standing with Mr. Brown and Ben's dad.

It was then that he saw Justin walking across the outfield, walking through the open door himself, coming over to where Ben stood behind the wall in left-center.

Now he was the one up-topping Ben with a high five.

"You okay?" Ben said to him, asking for a different reason than he'd asked Robbie.

"As Coop would say," Justin said, "I'm gorgeous."

"Really?"

"Really," he said. "You know how much I want to win. How much I wanted to win this. But I keep trying to feel like we lost, and I just can't."

"You got all of it."

"Almost all of it," he said. "But I couldn't let him walk me."

"Sometimes that's what sports is, you know?" Ben said. "It's almost."

"My dad always tells me to leave it all on the field," Justin said.

"All dads say that."

"But who knew," Justin said, "you could leave it *off* the field the way Robbie did?"

"Who knew?" Ben said.

They were silent for a moment and then Justin said, "Remember that night in my room when you asked me, what about my memories, how come they didn't count to my parents?"

Ben nodded.

"Thanks for helping me get one more," Justin said.

"Got a few myself," Ben said. "Just sayin'."

"I'll still never forget what you did for me," Justin said. "And the kind of friend you turned into."

"Same," Ben said.

Ben was going to say more. Was going to explain — one last time — that Justin had done more for him this season, way more. That as much as he thought he knew about being a teammate, and a friend, he'd found out you never stopped learning about how to be both.

Coop joked about not growing up, but maybe this was how you did, whether you wanted to or not, whether you were moving away or not.

Justin Bard said, "You know want to know something?"

"What?" Ben said.

And Justin said, "I'm ready to go now."

His friend knew exactly what he meant.

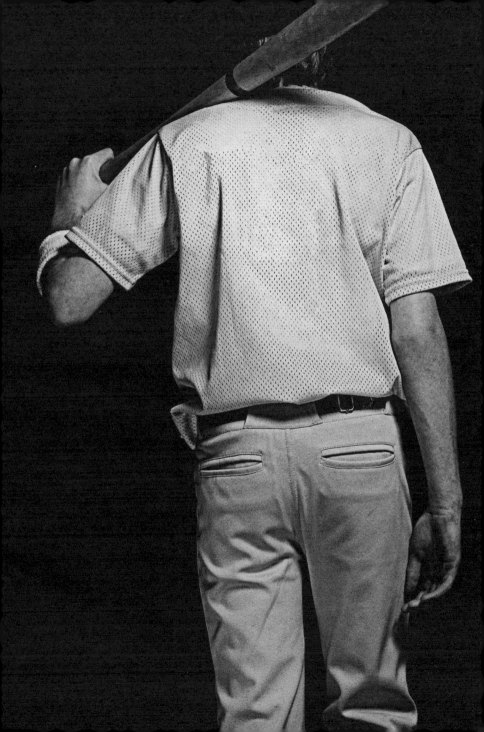

GAME CHANGERS

SEE HOW ONE INCREDIBLE FOOTBALL SEASON CHANGED THE GAME FOR BEN AND HIS FRIENDS.

Ben McBain is every football team's dream player. When the game is on the line, his number is the one being called for the final play. But Ben wants to be the starting quarterback and the one thing standing in his way is the coach's son.

Shawn O'Brien looks the part. He has been groomed by his father, a former professional quarterback. But despite his size and arm strength, Shawn is struggling.

Ben is torn between being a good teammate and going after his own dream. As Ben finds out, Shawn isn't the easiest person to help. And when Ben gets an unexpected opportunity, the entire game will change for the both of them.

ACKNOWLEDGMENTS

Thank you to my wife, Taylor, and our children: Christopher, Alex, Zach, and Hannah.

And thanks to all the kids I ever coached, and the memories they produced, and the stories they made me want to tell.